Then he started to box with Bert

The Bobbsey Twins
at Big Bear Pond

By

LAURA LEE HOPE

GROSSET & DUNLAP
Publishers   *New York*

The Bobbsey Twins at Big Bear Pond

CONTENTS

CHAPTER I

A STRANGE VISITOR

"FREDDIE! Flossie! Hurry up or we'll be late!"

Nan Bobbsey, a dark-haired, pretty girl of twelve, stood at the foot of the stairs, calling to her young brother and sister. Flossie and Freddie were twins and were six years old.

"I'm coming!" Flossie cried, and hurried down the stairs. "I don't want to be late for school, 'cause then you have to stay after and you can't have any fun."

The little blonde, curly-haired girl looked up at Nan with big blue eyes. Then Flossie called up the stairway for her twin. A moment later, a little boy who looked very much like her hurried down the stairs. Halfway down, he decided to ride the rest of the way, got astride the banister, and slid to the foot.

"I got here as soon as you did, Flossie," he said, and the three children went outside.

Reaching the street, they met Nan's twin brother, who was coming from the garage with his bicycle.

Bert, like Nan, was tall and slender, while Freddie and Flossie were plump. The two sets of twins started off down the street. Bert rode in the street along the curb and the others tried to keep up with him. As they passed a church they all looked up at the tower clock.

"We're not so late," said Flossie. "I don't like to hurry so I can't look at the scenery. It's such a bee-yoo-ti-ful day!"

"Yes, it is," Nan agreed. "I think spring is just about the nicest time of year anyhow."

About a block from the school, Freddie suddenly stopped. He pointed to some huge animal footprints in the soft earth alongside the sidewalk.

"Oo!" said Flossie. "An awful big dog must have made those."

"I'll bet it was an elephant," said Freddie, giggling.

As Freddie placed his small feet over two of the footprints, Bert got off his bicycle and came to look.

"No dog ever made these," he said, puzzled. "But there hasn't been any circus or animal show here. Nan, what do you suppose made these?"

Before Nan had a chance to answer him, another boy came up to the Bobbseys. It was Danny

"There's a lion loose in Lakeport!"

Rugg. Danny was a little older than Bert, and he was always teasing the smaller children.

"You'd better run, Flossie and Freddie!" said Danny. "There's a lion loose in Lakeport."

With this he ran off, and the little twins looked at each other fearfully. Then Nan said, "Don't believe Danny. I think these footprints were made by some child who had artificial feet which he put on over his shoes."

"Oh, you mean like flippers?" Freddie asked.

"Yes," said Nan. The small twins felt better.

The Bobbseys reached school just as the bell was ringing. The older twins said good-by to the younger ones, and all of them went to their classrooms.

When Miss Moore, Flossie and Freddie's teacher, took the roll, she noted that one pupil named Nada Bergen was absent. Flossie, too, wondered what had happened to Nada. The two little girls had become good friends that year.

"This morning we will start with local news," said Miss Moore. "Now who has some to tell?"

Freddie raised his hand and, when called upon, came to the front of the room. He described the huge footprints the twins had seen.

Miss Moore raised her eyebrows and said, "Freddie, could you draw a picture of one of the prints?"

Freddie picked up a piece of chalk, and began to make an outline as he remembered the footprint.

"Is that the actual size?" the teacher asked.

"Yes, it is, Miss Moore," the little boy replied.

"Can you fill it in?" Miss Moore suggested. "I mean, how many toes did this animal have?"

Freddie did not remember, but Flossie raised her hand. When the teacher nodded, the little girl came forward, picked up another piece of chalk, and put in five toes.

The teacher smiled. Then, turning to the class, she said, "I believe the Bobbsey twins really have made a discovery. This is the footprint of a bear."

"Bear!" all the children cried out.

Freddie and Flossie were startled themselves. When had the bear been there and where was he now?

"A bear's foot is very interesting," said Miss Moore. "It has five toes on each foot. Now dogs and cats have a different arrangement. They have five toes on their forepaws but only four toes on their hind feet. Did you know that?"

All the children said they had never noticed this. Miss Moore went on to say that a bear's toe has a long curved claw on it.

"The claw is blunt," she explained. "But it's a very good weapon just the same. A bear can claw a person and hurt him badly."

As Miss Moore went on to say that some bears are friendly and only harm people when they are annoyed or frightened, Flossie and Freddie saw Danny Rugg run past the open doorway to their classroom. A second later they heard a loud, roaring noise and were sure that Danny was trying to imitate a lion.

"Who did that?" Miss Moore asked.

The twins did not answer. The teacher hurried to the hall, but evidently saw no one outside. Apparently other teachers had rushed to their doorways, too.

"Whoever disturbed us with that dreadful noise should be punished," the children heard one of the other teachers say.

Freddie and Flossie looked at each other. Should they tell? Then Freddie shook his head. They decided not to be tattletales.

A few minutes later, Mr. Tetlow, the principal, came into their classroom. He said that since the disturbing, roaring noise had been just outside, perhaps one of the children had seen the person who was responsible.

"There have been too many disturbances in the school lately," the principal went on. "I'm going to get to the bottom of this!"

Still Freddie and Flossie kept silent. They wondered what to do. Finally they both decided that they did not know for sure that it was Danny who had made the noise. They only thought so, so they did not mention his name to Mr. Tetlow. The principal left the classroom and in a few minutes all the teachers returned to their rooms and work began again.

Several of Flossie and Freddie's classmates gave interesting bits of news. One had seen an exciting movie about the North Pole. Another had gone to watch firemen put out a fire in a store.

"And now," Miss Moore said, as the story ended, "we'll start our arithmetic."

As she turned toward the blackboard to write down some numbers, suddenly a little girl in the class screamed. Everyone looked at her. The child was pointing a trembling hand toward the door and everyone turned to look.

There stood a huge black bear on his hind legs!

CHAPTER II

HUGS DOES HIS TRICKS

THE PUPILS in Flossie and Freddie's class scattered in every direction. Some ran through the other door out of the classroom. Others hid under the desks. The little twins did not move but began to shake with fright. The big black bear lumbered toward them with a rolling gait. Flossie screamed then, and started to run toward the corner of the room.

"Wait!" a voice cried from behind the bear.

Freddie and Flossie had had several bad frights in their short lives. They had been having adventures ever since they were babies. Together with their older brother and sister, they had been on many trips and had visited the seashore, farms, mountains, cities and forests. Everywhere they had adventures. Just recently, they had spent some time at a strange, closed-up hotel and solved a mystery. This adventure was called THE BOBBSEY TWINS AND THE HORSESHOE RIDDLE.

Once, when they had gone to Rainbow Valley,

the twins had had fun with a bear. This one which had entered the classroom reminded Freddie and Flossie a little of that other bear. But seeing a big black animal in the woods and seeing one in a classroom were two different things.

"Wait, everybody!" the voice said again.

From behind the bear walked little Nada Bergen. In her hand was a chain attached to a collar around the bear's neck. None of the children had noticed the collar and chain, and naturally thought the bear had come in by himself.

"The bear won't hurt you," said Nada. "Hugs is very friendly."

The Bobbsey twins were the first to come forward. Slowly the other children came from beneath their desks, and those in the hall returned to their seats.

All this time Miss Moore had stood still by the blackboard. She, too, had been very frightened. But now she felt that the bear must be friendly, because he was walking on his hind legs as if he were putting on an act.

"Nada," she asked rather breathlessly, "where did you get such a big playmate?"

"Hugs belongs to my grandfather," the little girl replied. "It's because of Hugs that I didn't get here until late."

"Suppose you tell us about it," Miss Moore suggested.

Nada now told the class that her grandfather owned a piece of land in the woods. There was a pond in it which was called Big Bear Pond. He had set up a number of cages in which he kept tame bears.

"The bears don't stay in the cages all the time," said Nada. "My grandfather trains them for circuses and animal shows and lots of things. Hugs has just made a moving picture."

"How interesting!" Miss Moore remarked. "Where was this movie made?"

Nada said that the picture had been made some distance from Lakeport. Men who worked for her grandfather had been bringing Hugs back in a truck. They had come through Lakeport and stopped to see Nada's parents.

"We're going up to my grandfather's next week," said Nada, "so I begged the men to leave Hugs with me. My daddy said he would take him up in a truck when we go."

"Is he a trick bear?" Freddie called out.

"He certainly is," said Nada. "Would you like to see him do some tricks?"

"Yes, yes!" all the pupils begged.

Nada asked Miss Moore if it would be all right. When the teacher nodded, Nada led Hugs to the blackboard. She picked up a piece of chalk and wrote the number two on the board. Then she put another two under it and drew a line beneath it. Then Nada laid down the chalk.

"Now, Hugs," she said, "how much is two and two?" Nada put the chalk between two of Hugs' toes and he wrote a big four on the blackboard.

Miss Moore sent a message to Mr. Tetlow, the principal, asking him to come to her classroom. When he came, he was amazed to see Hugs and said sternly that it was against the rules for pets to be at school—particularly bears!

"But Hugs is very tame," said Miss Moore.

Nada, who was standing beside Hugs, turned

pale. A look of fright came over her face. Maybe Mr. Tetlow would expel her! Tears came to her eyes.

"Mr. Tetlow," said Miss Moore quickly, seeing the effect his words were having on Nada, "please give your permission for all the pupils in our school to see the bear perform. They will love him. He's a motion picture bear!"

"A motion picture bear, you say?" the principal repeated in astonishment. "Well, in that case, I suppose it might be a good idea. You arrange the little entertainment, Miss Moore."

As the teacher made the announcement to the class, Nada dried her eyes. Flossie came forward and put her arms around the little girl.

The class was permitted to go early to the playground. Freddie and Flossie walked down the corridor and into the school yard with Nada. On the way, Freddie asked what the tricks were which Hugs could perform. Freddie wanted to get the props for the bear. The little boy knew about props because he had been in a school play and knew that the furniture and various gadgets used in a play were called props.

"He can play ball," said Nada. "Will you get me a soft ball?"

Freddie hurried off to the gymnasium to ask the teacher there for a small soft ball.

"My bear can ride a bike," Nada told Flossie.

"Do you suppose we can borrow somebody's bike?"

"Bert rode his to school this morning," Flossie told her. "As soon as I see Bert come out, I'll go ask him."

Flossie stationed herself by the exit from which she knew Bert would come. The instant she saw her brother leave the building, she rushed up and told him the exciting news about Hugs. Then she asked Bert to get his bicycle quickly.

Bert went back into the building to bring out his bicycle. By the time he returned with it, a large circle of children had gathered about Hugs. Nada was explaining to them about her grandfather who lived at Big Bear Pond and trained circus and animal-show bears.

"Hugs and his sister are my favorites," said Nada. "Hugs' sister's name is Kisses."

The children laughed. Then they quieted down as the show started. Nada began giving commands. First she told Hugs to somersault. It seemed difficult for the bear to get down and roll over.

"He almost acts as if it hurt him," Flossie said anxiously.

While the bear was rolling over and over, Nada went up to Miss Moore and whispered to her. The teacher left the playground. While she was gone, Nada played ball with the bear. She was not very good at this, so Bert Bobbsey stepped forward and offered to help. Bert played a lot of baseball and could pitch very straight.

Hugs liked this game. He stood on his hind legs and batted the ball back with his paw. Then he started to box with Bert.

In a few moments Miss Moore returned with a portable radio. She tuned it until music began to play. At once Hugs started to dance. He did not just go around and around, as the Bobbseys and the other children had seen bears do. Hugs was far better than this. He did a step something like a polka, and presently Nada went up and danced with him.

"Oh, I want to do that!" Flossie cried.

Miss Moore looked at her wrist watch and said that they did not have too much time left.

"Suppose we let Hugs do all his tricks first, Flossie," she said. "Then if there is any time left, perhaps you can dance with the bear."

"Let's have Hugs ride the bicycle now," Nada suggested.

Hugs was very heavy and Nan was afraid that her twin's bicycle might crash when the bear sat on it. But nothing happened. Hugs sat astride the seat, put his feet on the pedals, and after Bert got him started, rode in a circle by himself.

Hugs completed the circle, then got off, letting the bicycle drop to the ground. He shook his head up and down as if he were bowing. All the children clapped loudly and asked for more tricks.

Suddenly Danny Rugg pushed his way through the group and walked up. He held a short whip in his hand.

"I'll show you how to make a bear do tricks," he boasted.

With that he cracked the whip in the air in front of the bear's face. Hugs stepped back.

"This is the way they do it in the circus," Danny shouted.

Now he swung the whip hard. He meant merely to whip the air, but instead, the whip cracked across the bear's nose with a resounding clap.

"Oh!" Flossie and Freddie and the others cried out.

Before Danny could move, Hugs growled menacingly and started for the boy.

CHAPTER III

A BEAR HUNT

"LOOK out! Run!" cried several teachers.

The children on the school playground pushed and tumbled over one another to get out of the way of the bear.

Meanwhile Bert Bobbsey had grabbed Danny Rugg's arm and tried to take the whip away from him. Danny, furious, cracked the whip and it came down across Bert's hand.

The lash stung and Bert winced with pain. Angry, he punched Danny hard. The other boy lost his balance and fell to the ground.

The fracas confused Hugs. He continued to growl, rearing up on his hind legs one moment, dropping to the earth the next.

"Hugs! Hugs!" Nada cried.

She put her arms tightly around his neck and kept telling him over and over that he must behave. She was fearful that Hugs would attack Danny Rugg.

Mr. Tetlow pushed his way through the mass

of screaming, frightened children. By the time he reached Hugs, Nada had managed to calm the bear.

"I thought you said this bear was tame," the principal said furiously. "Nada, it is inexcusable for you to have done such a thing. Take that bear over to the fence and chain him. Then come to my office. I'll telephone to your house for your father to come here and take the animal away immediately."

In the meantime Danny had picked himself up from the ground. He rushed at Bert, lashing out with his right arm. Bert ducked just in time to avoid a hard jab.

"Boys!" Mr. Tetlow shouted, rushing toward them. "Stop that fighting at once!"

"Bert started it," Danny whimpered.

Bert said nothing, but Freddie rushed up to defend his brother. "Mr. Tetlow, look at Bert's hand!" he cried. "Danny hit him with the whip!"

The principal gazed at the angry-looking welt on the back of Bert's hand. He set his jaw firmly and gave Danny a hard look. Then he said:

"Both of you boys come to my office at once. You know that it's against the rules to fight on the school grounds!"

He ordered all the other pupils to return to their classrooms. Before going into the building, Nan Bobbsey hurried over to the fence to help

Nada. The chain was a very heavy one and Nada assured Nan that the bear could not possibly get away.

"I'd better go to my class now," she said unhappily. "Daddy will be here soon to take Hugs home."

School finally settled down to a normal routine for everyone but Bert and Danny. Mr. Tetlow told them that the punishment he had meted out before to boys who had fought on the school grounds had not been very effective. He was going to try something different this time.

Bert and Danny wondered what it would be. They were amazed to learn that they were not to be allowed to go home during the lunch period. Mr. Tetlow said he would supply them with a sandwich and milk, but that the rest of the time they must work for him. Then they were to stay after school for an hour and do more work.

"Now return to your class," he said.

As the boys left the office, they heard Mr. Tetlow ask his secretary to put a call in to Nada Bergen's home. Glancing from a window, Bert saw Hugs tied to the fence. The bear was sitting down, looking at the cars going past him in the street.

"I'm not going back to class," said Danny. "If you don't tell, our teacher won't know how long Mr. Tetlow kept me."

"What are you going to do?" Bert asked him.

"I'm going outside and have some fun with Hugs."

Bert advised him strongly not to do this. He even suggested that some teacher might look out the window and see Danny. She would certainly report him.

"I'm going to take a chance," said Danny. "Anyhow my head hurts from that punch you gave me. I can't study."

Without another word Danny hurried out a side door. Bert went to his classroom. When his teacher asked where Danny was, Bert said that Danny had a headache. This made everyone in the class laugh, because they had all seen the good punch Bert had given Danny.

When the dismissal bell sounded at noontime, Bert told Nan that he had to stay at school, and asked her to tell their mother. Nan nodded. As she left the school building, she noticed that Hugs was gone.

"Mr. Bergen must have come for him," she thought.

Nan and the small twins were seated at their luncheon when the telephone rang. Nan hurried to answer it. Freddie and Flossie heard her say:

"Oh, Nada, that's dreadful!"

"What's dreadful?" Freddie cried, jumping up.

"We certainly will try to help you find him," Nan said into the telephone.

"Find whom?" Flossie called out.

In a few moments Nan hung up and came to tell Freddie and Flossie what Nada had said.

"Hugs is gone! When Mr. Bergen got to the school, the bear was not there!"

"What happened to him?" Flossie asked, wide-eyed.

"Nobody knows," Nan replied. "Nada thinks he's been stolen!"

"Oh!" Freddie and Flossie exclaimed together.

Nan went on to say that Nada and her parents were very upset. Of course it was possible that Hugs had pulled loose from the fence and wandered off.

"Nada wants us to help her find Hugs," Nan told the small twins.

"And we'll sure do it!" said Freddie.

Mrs. Bobbsey, a slender, pretty woman who was seated at the table with them, smiled at the children. She said it would be a very exciting adventure to try to find a missing bear. But she warned them not to be disappointed if they were not successful.

"By the time school is over, I'm afraid Hugs may be many miles away from here," she said.

This gave Nan an idea. She said, "Do you suppose Mr. Tetlow would excuse us this afternoon, so we can hunt for the bear?"

Her mother said she thought this was hardly likely, but it would not hurt to ask him. She suggested that Nan call the principal at once and talk with him.

"Tell him Flossie and I want to go, too!" Freddie said.

Nan also had another idea. Bert had told her why Danny had not come back to the classroom. It was just possible that the bully, to get even, had let the bear go. Or he might have taken him to his own house.

But when Nan talked to Mr. Tetlow on the telephone, she did not tell him that she suspected Danny. She merely asked if she might take a little time off to help Nada hunt for Hugs.

"Freddie and Flossie want to go with me," she said. "You know Nada is one of Flossie's friends."

At first Mr. Tetlow did not see how it was possible for him to grant permission. He said he was afraid that if he should let Nan and the small twins have time off from class, he would be deluged with requests from other pupils.

"But, Mr. Tetlow, Hugs may be in trouble," Nan pleaded. "I'll make up any work I miss, and Flossie and Freddie will, too. I'll help them."

Mr. Tetlow chuckled. "All right," he said. "You've convinced me. But try to get back to school sometime during the afternoon if you possibly can."

"Oh, thank you, Mr. Tetlow," Nan said happily.

She hurried back to the table to tell the small twins the good news. It was decided that the search would start at Danny's house. If Hugs was not there, they would go to Nada's home.

When the children reached Danny's, Hugs was not in sight, nor was he in the garage.

Danny's mother came outside to ask what they were searching for, and Nan explained. She also told Mrs. Rugg that Danny would not be home until late because he and Bert were being punished for the fight at school. Nan did not mention her suspicion that Danny might have been responsible for Hugs' disappearance.

As the children walked toward Nada's house, they saw the truck from their father's lumberyard coming down the street. Sam, who worked for Mr. Bobbsey, was driving it.

"Sam, stop!" Freddie cried out. "Have you seen a big black bear?"

"Why, as a matter of fact, I have!" Sam called, bringing the truck to a stop. Sam, an elderly colored man with a wonderful smile, was always ready to help the twins solve a mystery.

Sam explained that he had seen a van in front of a lakeport diner. Two men and a boy had been looking at a bear inside the van.

"Oh, that must be Hugs!" Flossie cried. "Somebody's stolen him!"

Nan quickly explained about Nada Bergen's missing bear, and Sam scratched his head. He agreed that the bear he had seen might indeed have been stolen.

"Suppose you all hop up in here," he said, "and we'll go take a look!"

"Let's pick up Nada," Flossie begged. "She'll know if the bear is Hugs."

"All right," Sam agreed.

CHAPTER IV

A BAD DAY FOR BERT

AS SAM drove Mr. Bobbsey's lumber truck toward the diner where he had seen the horse van with a bear in it, Nada and the twins asked him a hundred questions. Was the bear happy? Or did he look sad? Was he growling and did he act as if he wanted to get out?

Sam chuckled. "You children can ask more questions than a lawyer. I can't rightly tell you anything about that bear. I don't suppose I would have thought twice about it, except you don't expect to find a bear in a horse van."

The Bobbsey children could hardly wait to reach the diner. In a few minutes Sam wrinkled his brow.

"Is something the matter?" asked Flossie, who saw Sam frown.

"The horse van's gone," he said, looking ahead.

Nevertheless, he pulled up in front of the

diner. He said it might be a good idea to go inside and find out how long the van had been gone. He climbed down and went into the restaurant.

"Oh, maybe Hugs is gone forever!" Nada wailed. "And if bad men have Hugs, they may hurt him!"

Nan asked Nada to try to stop worrying. She was sure they would find the horse van with the bear in it.

A second later, Sam came out of the diner. He smiled at the children and said the van had not been gone very long and that it had taken the road on which they were traveling.

"We'll catch it," he said cheerfully.

Sam climbed back into the cab and started off once more. He put on a little more speed and about ten minutes later Freddie cried out:

"I see it! There's the horse van just ahead."

Sam tooted his horn as he came alongside the van, and motioned the driver to pull over to the side of the road. But the driver did not pull over. Instead, he waved his hand, motioning for Sam to fall behind.

On the seat beside the driver was another man. But the boy Sam had mentioned was not with them. The children wondered if he might be inside the van with the bear.

The two vehicles continued to run along the road side by side. Sam had refused to fall behind and the driver of the horse van had refused to stop.

"Oh, what will we do?" Flossie asked.

Nan called out the window to the man, "We have to talk to you a minute."

"What about?" the driver asked her.

"About the bear you're carrying."

"Well, what about it? He belongs to us and we're taking him where we want to." The man was not very pleasant.

"If the bear belongs to you, why do you mind letting us see him?" Nan went on.

"Because I'm in a hurry," the man replied.

The situation was getting worse and worse. It might have had an unfortunate ending, but just at that moment, a trooper from the State Police Headquarters came toward them on a motorcycle. Seeing him coming, Sam fell behind the horse van. But when the trooper reached him, Sam leaned out and said:

"Officer, we think that bear in the van ahead of us may have been stolen."

"You mean it might be the missing Hugs?" the policeman asked. "We've been alerted to be on the watch for him."

"Yes."

Nan spoke up. "We tried to make the man stop and let us see the bear, but he wouldn't do it. Won't you help us?"

The officer said he certainly would, and told

Sam to follow him. He turned his motorcycle around and roared off up the road after the horse van. Sam put on more speed and followed.

"Now we're going to get those bad men!" Freddie cried, jumping up and clapping his hands.

Nan warned her small brother that the men might not be bad at all. He must be very careful what he said to them. Freddie promised, but he was sure in his own mind that they were going to get Hugs back.

The officer had already stopped the driver of the horse van. By the time Sam drew up and they all climbed out, the policeman had made the men open the back of the van. The bear was tied by his collar to each side of the van so that he could hardly move. Nada hopped up into the van and looked closely at the bear.

"Well, are you satisfied?" the driver asked sarcastically.

Nada just stood and stared. Finally she said, "This bear isn't Hugs, but he looks an awful lot like the ones my grandfather has at Big Bear Pond."

As she said this, Nan thought the two men looked a bit frightened. But a second later she decided she must be wrong. What would they be frightened about? If this was not Hugs, then they had probably told the truth when they said that the bear in the van belonged to them.

"Well, officer," said the driver, "I suppose it's

all right for us to go on now. Children get funny ideas in their heads. They've wasted fifteen minutes of our good time."

All this time the other man was staring intently at Nada Bergen. Finally he asked who she was. When the little girl gave her name, the man frowned.

"Where do you live?" he demanded.

"In Lakeport," Nada replied. "But I spend lots of time with my grandfather at Big Bear Pond."

"I see," the man said.

Something about the way the man made his last remark bothered Nan. Why should he ask Nada all these questions? Finally Nan said to the man:

"Do you know Nada's grandfather, Mr. Bergen, who trains bears?"

"I don't know him, but I've heard of him," the man replied. "Well, come on, Joe, we've wasted enough time already."

"You're right, Al," the driver said.

As they moved off, Flossie spoke up. "What's the name of your boy?"

The two men looked puzzled. Then Flossie explained she was talking about the boy who had been seen with them at the diner.

"Oh, that's Biff Rand," the driver said. "He likes to ride with us sometimes. We left him in Lakeport."

They climbed into their van and drove off.

Nada and the Bobbseys got back into the cab of the lumber truck, and Sam drove them back into town.

"Where shall I take you all?" he asked.

"Please leave us at school, Sam," Nan suggested. "I guess we'll have to give up the search for Hugs."

When Freddie and Flossie and Nada reached their classroom, Miss Moore asked them to tell the class what they had found out. Flossie and Freddie told about their ride out of town to the horse van and how there had been another bear in it. Nada said that her father had notified the police, but Hugs had not yet been found by them.

"I'm going to hunt some more after school," said Nada.

Flossie and Freddie declared that they were, too, and every pupil in the class said he would help hunt.

When the final bell rang, the small children all hurried off. They would report home first, then start their search.

In Nan and Bert's classroom, there was a different conversation going on. Danny Rugg had not returned to the school, and everyone was very suspicious that he had gone off with the bear.

"I wish I could go hunt for both Danny and the bear," Bert said to his twin, "but I have to stay after school for an hour and work for Mr. Tetlow."

"I'm sorry," said Nan. "I suppose Mr. Tetlow has to punish people who disobey the school rules, but I think you had a right to punch Danny. How's your hand feeling?"

"It aches a little bit," Bert confessed, "but I guess it will be all right soon."

The twins separated and Bert went off to report to Mr. Tetlow. The principal was angry that Danny had run off. He said Danny would certainly be severely punished for what he had done.

"I'm glad to see that you're taking your punishment like a man, Bert," the principal said, smiling. "Well, let's get to work. I want you to take that big pile of letters over there and sort them alphabetically. When you get through with that job, you're to go around to all the classrooms and clean off the blackboards."

Bert wished that Mr. Tetlow would give him a more entertaining job, but he did not complain.

"You must work exactly one hour," the principal said. "At the end of that time, come back and report to me."

"Yes, sir," Bert said.

He started sorting the letters, and in about fifteen minutes went off to clean the blackboards. As he went from room to room, it seemed to him as if the hour would never be up. But as he came to the last room, he noticed that the clock was just turning to four.

"Oh well, I may as well do this blackboard anyway," Bert told himself and got to work.

He finished it quickly and reported to Mr. Tetlow's office. Then he started for the basement to get his bicycle. Suddenly he remembered that he had never brought it back from the playground after he had lent it for Hugs' performance.

Bert hurried from the building and went at once to the playground. The bicycle was not in sight.

"Somebody must have taken it inside for me," Bert told himself.

He returned to the building and went to the section of the cellar where the boys kept their bicycles. His was not there. He walked over to the place where the girls' bicycles were kept. It was not there either.

A strange feeling came over Bert. He went from one place to another in the building. Then he rushed outdoors, going all the way around the school grounds. His bicycle was not to be found.

"Somebody's stolen it!" Bert Bobbsey thought fearfully.

CHAPTER V

TWO BOYS IN A TREE

FOR several seconds Bert Bobbsey stood still on the school grounds and just stared into space. He was both angry and sad about the loss of his bicycle.

There was no question in his mind but that someone had taken it. Was it just a joke and would he get it back? Or had someone really stolen it?

The bicycle meant a lot to Bert. He had earned the money to help pay for it and it was a very fine one with all sorts of special gadgets on it. Among them were head and tail lights of special glass.

"I'm going to get that bike of mine back!" Bert determined.

As he walked up the street, he decided to find his friend Charlie Mason. He and Charlie often solved little mysteries together. Moreover, Charlie had an old bicycle which Bert knew he could borrow.

When Bert reached Charlie's house, he went around to the back yard where his friend was working on a midget car. Charlie was a good-looking boy about Bert's size. He had large brown eyes and a pleasant smile.

"Hi, Bert!" he called. "What's up?"

"Your car's nifty," said Bert.

Then he explained that his bicycle had been stolen. "I thought if you'd lend me your old bike, and you ride your regular one, we could cover Lakeport together and try to locate mine."

Charlie agreed to the plan immediately. Bert helped him pick up all his tools and run the midget car into the garage. Then they set off on

Charlie's two bicycles. They rode up one street and down another without finding any clues to Bert's missing bike. Both boys stopped several times to ask people on the street if they had seen a good-looking new bicycle with special head and tail lights. But no one had.

After a while Charlie chuckled. "Bert," he said, "you don't suppose Danny Rugg took it, do you? He didn't come back to school. Maybe he's off having a nice time on your bike."

Bert said he thought everyone suspected Danny of having taken Hugs. It had not occurred to him that Danny might also have helped himself to the bicycle.

"Let's go to Danny's house and see what we can find out," he said.

They found Danny sitting on his front porch steps. He looked very glum and did not glance up until the boys were almost in front of him.

"What's eating you, Danny?" Charlie asked him. "Are you afraid to come back to school?"

Danny's look of glumness changed to one of anger. His eyes flashed, as he said:

"I'm not afraid of Mr. Tetlow or anybody else!"

Danny then began a long speech on how sick and tired he was of people picking on him. He was not going to take orders from Bert Bobbsey or his family or anybody else.

"My mother said your dumb sisters and

brother were over here saying I took the bear!"
Danny shouted.

He got up from the steps glowering, and
looked as if he might start another fight with
Bert. The Bobbsey twin almost wished he would.
Nothing would have given him more pleasure
at that moment than to thrash Danny good and
proper for his mean remarks.

"If my sisters and brother asked your mother
about the bear, it was because they had good
reason to," he said. "You left the school, and
right after that Hugs disappeared."

Danny looked a little frightened, but he at
once denied knowing anything about the bear.
He admitted being angry because Mr. Tetlow
was going to punish him, and he had stayed away
from school to avoid it. He was going to get his
father to go with him the next morning to see the
principal. He was not going to stand such treatment!

Bert and Charlie smiled. They knew it would
do no good for Mr. Rugg to talk to the principal.
Mr. Tetlow was very firm with his pupils and
had a reputation for fairness. Danny's reputation in the school, on the other hand, was not so
enviable.

"Maybe you didn't take the bear," said Bert,
"but something else has disappeared from the
school playground, too. I'm here to ask you what
you know about it."

"Well, whatever it is, I don't know anything about it," said Danny quickly.

"Okay, Danny," said Bert. "What disappeared is my bicycle. I left it on the playground after Hugs had ridden on it. Did you see anyone pick it up?"

"I certainly didn't," said Danny. "When I left the school, I went out the door at the other end of the building."

At this moment the front door opened. Mrs. Rugg came out and said that Danny's supper was ready. She nodded to the other two boys.

"Mother," said Danny, "Bert Bobbsey is saying I stole his bicycle."

"What!" Mrs. Rugg cried.

Bert explained that he had not accused Danny of stealing the bicycle. He had merely asked him if he knew anything about it.

"Well, you'd better not accuse my son of being a thief!" said Mrs. Rugg haughtily, and ushered her son into the hall and closed the front door.

Bert and Charlie went off. With a sigh, Bert said perhaps they had better give up trying to find the bicycle, at least for today.

"Suppose we ride over to the woods outside of town and look around for Hugs," he suggested.

"A swell idea," Charlie agreed.

When the boys reached the woods, they hid their bicycles in a cave not far from the road. They walked along the trail, listening and watching for any signs of the missing bear. The only things they saw or heard were squirrels and a couple of rabbits. Then suddenly they heard something crashing through the underbrush. A few seconds later a frightened deer leaped almost past them, jumping in huge strides.

"Something must have frightened him," Bert said.

He had hardly spoken when he heard a dog barking. Presently a large, vicious-looking dog burst from a small clearing and raced after the deer.

Bert knew that should the dog catch up to the deer, he would injure it badly—perhaps fatally.

"Hey, cut that out!" he cried.

When the dog did not stop, Bert picked up a stone and threw it far ahead of the dog to frighten him. The stone landed with a thud and accomplished what Bert wanted it to. The ugly dog stopped short in his tracks.

But instantly he turned around to see where the stone had come from. Spying the two boys, the dog made a beeline for them. There was no question but that he would attack them.

"Run!" Charlie cried.

"We'd better climb a tree," Bert suggested.

It was some distance to trees stout enough to climb. As the two boys raced toward the nearest one, the dog doubled his speed toward them.

Could Bert and Charlie get to safety in time?

CHAPTER VI

FREDDIE'S RIDE

CHARLIE, who was nearest the tree, got there first and shinned up. Fortunately for Bert, the ugly dog was running so fast that he could not avoid a slippery stone. It made him somersault in the air. By the time the dog landed on his feet and continued his race toward the tree, Bert had climbed to the lowest branch.

"Wowie!" Bert panted. "That sure was close!"

The dog leaped against the tree trunk, yelping and barking loudly.

"Take it easy, old fellow," Bert advised him, grinning. "We put one over on you that time."

But the dog had no intention of taking it easy. He continued to run around the tree, whining and snarling because he could not get at them.

It seemed to the waiting boys as if the dog would never stop. But in about ten minutes, he evidently decided that his captives were not coming down. He started to walk off.

"Hurray! He's going!" Charlie said gleefully.

"That's what you think," said Bert, as the dog turned back, looked at the tree, and then flopped down on the ground. He was merely having a rest, with both eyes lifted toward the boys. Any move on their part and the dog would be at them again.

"Say, what are we going to do?" Charlie asked a few minutes later. "We can't stay up here all night."

"You're right," Bert agreed. He began to try to figure out a way to outwit the dog. Charlie did the same.

"We might throw some things at a distance for the old fellow to retrieve," he suggested. "While he's gone, we might climb down and run."

"We can't lose by trying," Bert grinned. Both boys broke off pieces of a branch above them and threw them far beyond the dog. He merely cocked an ear and did not even get up.

"Let's start yelling for help," Charlie next suggested.

The two boys shouted as loudly as they could, over and over, but no one came to help them out of their predicament. Suddenly Charlie had another idea.

"I'll tell you what," he said. "Suppose one of us starts down on one side of the tree, just to pretend we're leaving. Then the other one can climb down the other side and sneak off."

Bert was afraid this would not work. He reminded Charlie of the keen sense of smell which dogs have and their highly sensitive hearing. He doubted whether they could fool the animal this way.

"I have an idea," said Bert.

Not far from the large tree in which the boys were seated was a sapling. Around the trunk of this tree, a heavy vine had wound itself up and up. Some distance up, the vine stretched to the tree in which Charlie and Bert were waiting.

"Let's take that vine and braid it into a rope," Bert suggested.

"And tie up the dog?" Charlie asked.

"Yes."

"But how?" Charlie said. "That dog could give you an awful bite while you're trying to tie him up."

"Oh, we can think of something if we can only make the rope," said Bert.

He climbed higher in the tree and began to unwind the vine from the branches. Charlie followed and started with another one. To their delight the vine did not pull apart when they yanked on it.

It was slow work but after a while the boys

Bert lassoed the vicious dog

had several twelve-foot lengths of the vine. Then, after braiding them tightly, the rope was finished. "Now what?" Charlie asked.

"I'm going to try to lasso him," Bert explained, adding that this should keep the dog quiet until they could get down and tie him properly.

A loop was fashioned and Bert swung it round and round, dropping it toward the dog. As the animal leaped up, the lasso swung around his neck and Bert gave it a jerk. Frightened, the dog yanked and strained, almost pulling the boys from the tree, but they held on, and wound the rope around a branch.

Instantly the boys shinned down the tree. Then Bert picked up a big branch with leaves on it and handed this to Charlie. While his friend waved the branch in the dog's face, Bert slipped up, removed the lasso and tied it to the dog's collar.

"Run!" Bert cried, and the two boys dashed through the woods. When they were a safe distance away, they turned and saw the dog gnawing steadily at the vine rope.

"It will take him awhile to bite through that," Charlie said, laughing, as the boys reached their bicycles and headed for home.

Back in Lakeport, Freddie Bobbsey was about to start off on a search of his own. He was telling Sam's wife, Dinah, the family cook, about Hugs' strange disappearance.

"Dinah, how long will it be before supper is ready?" Freddie had asked.

"Half an hour," Dinah had replied.

"Then I'm going out on my two-wheeler for half an hour and hunt for Hugs," Freddie announced.

"All right," said Dinah. "But listen, honey child, you take mighty good care of yourself. It's beginning to get a little dark. You stay right on the sidewalk."

"I will," said Freddie. "I'll just go all around the block. Okay?"

"Okay, but don't you be late for your supper," said Dinah. "I have something special that you like."

"What is it?" Freddie asked eagerly.

"Well, it's something bears like, too," Dinah replied, smiling. "It's cinnamon cake made with molasses."

Freddie paused long enough to say that he would certainly be back in time for supper. Then he remarked that bears never got cinnamon cake with molasses in the woods. What did they eat out there?

"Oh, lots of things," said Dinah. She laughed. "They like to eat bumblebees and hornets!"

"And they don't get stung?" Freddie asked in amazement.

Dinah shook her head. She went on to say that

bears also liked to eat centipedes, those crawly little bugs with hundreds of legs.

"And they like to eat frogs and toads and field mice. One thing they like for dessert is ants," the cook said. "You know what Old Mr. Bear does to get ants?"

"No. What?"

"Well," said Dinah, "Mr. Bear runs his four legs deep down into an ant hill. That makes the ants pretty angry and they run out. And then Old Mr. Bear eats them all up."

Freddie paused in the doorway. He told Dinah he was sure he would not like to eat a bear's dinner. Then he ran to the garage to get his two-wheeler and set off down the street.

After he turned the corner, Freddie looked left and right for Hugs as he went along. He did not see any sign of the bear, and turned the next corner. By the time Freddie was halfway down the block, it was growing pretty dark. It would be hard to see Hugs now, he decided.

His thoughts turned once more to a bear's diet. How in the world could he get hold of bumblebees and hornets without being stung?

Freddie was busy trying to think this out, when suddenly something struck him from behind. The little boy flew off his bicycle and landed in the street. He hit his head hard and everything went black.

CHAPTER VII

HUGS IS BLAMED

NOT FAR from where Freddie Bobbsey lay unconscious in the street, was Nellie Parks' house. Nellie was a friend of Nan's and at this moment the two girls were standing on the front porch of the house, saying good night.

"We'll hunt for Hugs some more tomorrow," said Nellie.

"As soon as school is over," said Nan. Then, after a pause, she added, "Goodness, a bear's so big you can't hide him just anywhere."

Nellie agreed. She said certainly Hugs should be found soon.

Nan walked down the flagstone path to the street. Then she turned toward her own home. She had gone only part way up the block when her eyes nearly popped from her head. On the sidewalk lay an overturned bicycle—and in the street, just beyond the curbstone, was a little boy lying face down.

"Oh, my goodness!" Nan cried.

She ran forward to help the child. To her complete horror, she saw that it was her own little brother!

"Freddie! Freddie!" she cried fearfully, turning him slightly.

Freddie did not answer. His eyes were closed and blood was oozing from a cut on the back of his head.

Nan picked Freddie up flat in her arms, knowing from her first-aid work that it was best to keep him lying flat. The little boy was heavy, but she did not think of this.

"I'd better take him to Nellie's," Nan told herself.

She wished someone would come along to help her, but there was no one near by at the moment. She struggled along the street with her burden and finally came to the Parks' home. She managed to get to their porch and ring the bell.

Nellie opened the door. She gave a cry of dismay.

"Oh, Nan, what happened?"

Nan did not reply. She walked into the Parks' home and lay Freddie on a couch in the living room. By this time Nellie had called her mother and Mrs. Parks came on the run.

"I—I found Freddie lying in the street," said Nan, starting to sob. "Please telephone for Dr. Badgely. And call my mother."

Mrs. Parks rushed off to do this. Nan asked Nellie please to bring cold water and a towel. Meanwhile, she gently stroked Freddie's forehead and rubbed his wrists.

When Nellie brought water and towels, Nan bathed the cut on Freddie's head and then put a fresh cold towel on his forehead. Then she massaged Freddie's face and rubbed his arms. Presently his eyelids began to flicker and he opened his eyes for a moment.

"He's coming to!" Nan said eagerly.

The doorbell rang and Nellie hurried to answer it. Dr. Badgely had arrived. He came into the living room at once and began to examine Freddie without waiting to hear what had happened.

From his pocket the physician took a little case and emptied a couple of pills into the palm of his hand. He asked Nellie to bring a glass of water and also an empty glass. When she got them, Dr. Badgely put the two little tablets into one and poured a bit of the water on them. They foamed up a bit. Then, holding Freddie's head gently, the doctor poured the liquid between his lips. Freddie gulped and suddenly opened his eyes wide.

"There, little man, you'll be all right," Dr. Badgely said kindly. "You had a bad tumble. No, just lie quiet," he added as Freddie tried to sit up. "I want to bandage your head."

The physician now asked Nan what had happened to her small brother. She said she did not know and told of how she had found Freddie.

"It's evident," said Dr. Badgely, "that something hit Freddie hard from behind. Something sharp cut the back of his head."

Mrs. Parks remarked that it was certainly dreadful when people left the scene of an accident. To think of hitting the little fellow and leaving him unconscious!

At this moment the doorbell rang again. This time it was Mr. and Mrs. Bobbsey and Flossie. They all rushed into the living room to see Freddie.

"Oh, my poor little boy!" Mrs. Bobbsey cried, kneeling on the floor beside the couch.

Freddie smiled wanly. "I'm all right, Mommy," he half-whispered.

Mr. Bobbsey asked Dr. Badgely if it would be all right to move Freddie to their own home at once. He said yes, if it were done carefully. He wanted the little boy to remain lying flat and not to be joggled.

Flossie, who had been standing wide-eyed all the time, now burst into tears. She grabbed hold of the doctor's hand and looked at him with pleading eyes.

"Freddie's my very own twin," she said, sobbing. "You mustn't let anything happen to him!"

The physician smiled and patted the little girl

on the head. "Nothing more is going to happen to Freddie," he assured her. "He's going to be all right, but he has to keep quiet and stay in bed."

Mrs. Parks spoke up, saying that they had a light rattan couch which was easy to carry. She suggested that Freddie be laid on this and carried to his own home.

Mr. Bobbsey went with her to get the couch. It was brought into the living room and Freddie was lifted onto it. Then the little parade started for the Bobbsey home. As the little boy was carried into the house, Dinah and Sam threw up their hands in horror. Quickly Flossie told them that her twin was going to be all right.

By the time Freddie was tucked into his own bed, he said he felt a little better. Dr. Badgely asked him a few questions about what had happened, but Freddie said that he did not know what had hit him.

"I think you should notify the police, Mr. Bobbsey," the doctor said.

The twins' father went to the telephone at once to notify Captain Roscoe.

While he was talking, Bert came into the house. Overhearing what his father was saying, the boy rushed up the stairs to see Freddie. He and Bert shared the same bedroom.

Freddie was glad to see his older brother but

did not feel like talking. He said he felt sick to his stomach whenever he moved.

"You just lie still, Freddie," Bert said. "And don't worry," he added fiercely. "I'm going to find out who hit you, right now!"

Bert came downstairs and asked Nan to show him the place where Freddie had had his accident. Sam overheard him and said he would like to go along, too.

Just before they came to the spot, a car with bright headlights drove down the street. It lighted up the scene brightly.

"There's somebody looking already," said Nan.

A boy with a flashlight was beaming it around the ground. Presently he stooped and picked something up.

"That's the boy who was with those men who had the bear," said Sam.

The boy heard their voices. Instantly he turned off the flashlight and ran.

"Hey, wait a minute!" Bert cried. It had occurred to him that the boy might have picked up a valuable clue to the person who had hit Freddie.

But Biff Rand did not stop. The others wondered why but soon forgot it.

When they reached the spot, Bert beamed his flashlight around the sidewalk. To their surprise it looked as if someone had deliberately tried to cover up any tracks or footprints. Dirt had been kicked from the edge of the walk and scattered over the sidewalk. Any marks which Freddie's two-wheel bicycle might have made were now gone.

Bert shrugged and they started back toward

the house. Halfway there, however, he said he wondered if by any chance Biff was responsible for running into Freddie and had come back to try to cover up any evidence.

When they reached the house, Flossie offered to stay with Freddie while the others ate supper. But Sam said he would like to sit beside Freddie and watch him.

By this time it was way past the supper hour, and Flossie had to admit that she was hungry. So she smiled at Sam and said she would come and relieve him as soon as she had finished eating.

It was nearly eight o'clock when supper was over. As the family arose from the table, and Mr. Bobbsey and his son stood back to let Mrs. Bobbsey, Nan, and Flossie leave the dining room, the front doorbell rang.

Flossie ran to open the door. There stood Nada Bergen and her father. It was very evident that the little girl had been crying, and her father looked worried. As they stepped into the hall, Nada cried out:

"How's Freddie?"

"He's getting better," said Flossie.

"Oh, I'm so glad," Nada said. Then she grabbed Flossie's hand and wailed, "Do you know what everybody is saying? That it was Hugs that hurt Freddie! Oh, Flossie, if the police find the bear, they're going to put him in jail!"

CHAPTER VIII

FLOSSIE'S VISIT

A BEAR in jail!

"Nada, what do you mean?" Nan Bobbsey asked the little girl.

Fighting to keep back the tears, Nada explained that the police had come to see her father and said that several calls had come in reporting people thought Hugs was in the neighborhood.

"But even if Hugs is," the little girl said, "he wouldn't hurt anybody. He's tame and he's friendly. He didn't even do anything to Danny Rugg when Danny was mean to him."

Mr. Bergen explained that the police had told him Hugs would be kept at headquarters—as soon as they found him—until everything was straightened out.

"But, Daddy," said Nada, "the policeman said they would put Hugs in a cell. That's where bad people go and Hugs isn't that!"

Mr. Bergen put his arm around his small daughter comfortingly. The police, he said, had

to be very careful and track down every clue.
But they would not harm the bear, so Nada was
to stop worrying.

"What is more important at the moment,"
said her father, "is to find out how Freddie is. I
hope he's going to be all right."

Mrs. Bobbsey, who had come forward, assured Mr. Bergen that her small son was gaining
his strength rapidly. It had been a dreadful scare
for all of them and she was very thankful that
Freddie was no worse off than he was.

"Since no one saw what happened to him,"
she said, "the whole thing is a great mystery.
Even if Hugs did attack him, I certainly shall
not blame you. Nan told me that your bear was
securely chained to the school fence. It is very
unlikely that he got himself loose. I'm sure someone unchained him."

"It will be a great relief to me and my wife
when Hugs has been captured," said Mr.
Bergen.

"But if he was stolen," Bert spoke up, "he may
never be found."

This remark made Nada burst into tears. Bert
was sorry that he had said anything. He told
Nada that even though the bear might have been
stolen, this did not mean that he would be treated
unkindly.

"Whoever took him, probably intended to sell
Hugs," he said.

"But I want him back!" Nada said.

Seeing how upset his daughter was, Mr. Bergen asked Mrs. Bobbsey if she would permit Flossie to spend the night with Nada. The two little girls had made several overnight trips to each other's house during the past few months and always had a great deal of fun together.

"Would you like to go, Flossie?" her mother asked.

Flossie clapped her hands and said she would love to. Would Nada come up to her bedroom with her while she packed her little suitcase?

The two little girls went up the stairway, tiptoeing so as not to disturb Freddie. Flossie put a nightie and robe and fresh clothes for the next day in her suitcase. But what she thought much more important was taking some of her dolls and dolls' clothes along. In the end she chose one large and two small dolls. Nada helped her select the right nightie and school clothes for the next day.

Finally Flossie closed the lid of the bag and snapped the locks. Then, picking it up, she followed Nada from the room and down the stairs.

"Have a nice time, dear," Mrs. Bobbsey said, as she kissed her little girl good night.

Nan got Flossie's coat from the hall closet and helped her into it. Then the visitors and their overnight guest left the house. By this time Nada had forgotten her troubles, and all the way to her house the two little girls giggled about first one thing and then another.

After they had put on their night clothes, Mrs. Bergen let them play for a little while. But finally she told them that they must climb into bed and go to sleep.

Nada's bedroom was very pretty and had little twin cots in it. Flossie was to sleep in one near a window. Mrs. Bergen listened as they said their prayers, then opened the window nearest Flossie.

The two little girls soon fell asleep. For a while Flossie slept soundly, then she became restless. Finally she woke up. For a moment she could not remember where she was. This was a strange place and moonlight was streaming into her eyes.

Suddenly Flossie shivered a little. She had heard a scratching sound against the house outside. She listened carefully. As the sound was repeated, Flossie became excited.

"Maybe that's Hugs scratching to get in!" she thought. "That's the same kind of sound Snap or Waggo make when they want to come into our house."

Snap and Waggo were the Bobbseys' two dogs. Snap was very old now and liked to sleep a good deal. Waggo was a young fox terrier who was very frisky. They stayed in their kennel in the Bobbseys' back yard most of the time, but once in a while they were allowed to roam. Usually

It was kind of spooky!

they wanted to come into the house for a treat. The sound Flossie had just heard sounded like their scratching on the back door.

Hearing it again, Flossie awakened Nada, who agreed that perhaps Hugs had come home. The two little girls put on robes and slippers and started down the stairway. The house was dark and the stairs creaked. It was kind of spooky!

"Maybe it's not Hugs!" Nada whispered. "Maybe it's a burglar!"

Doubtful herself now, Flossie led the way to a back window and peered out. No one was there! Tiptoeing to the front of the house they checked the front door. But again, no one was there. Just then they heard the scratching sound once more!

"Maybe Hugs is on the roof and trying to get down the chimney!" Flossie suggested.

Nada laughed, saying Hugs was pretty large to squeeze down a chimney, but she decided to ask her father and mother to investigate.

Flossie waited in the hall while Nada awoke her mother. Mrs. Bergen listened carefully, then Flossie heard her say, "Why, Nada dear, that's just a branch from the big maple tree scratching the house!"

She got out of bed and for the second time that night tucked the little girls in bed, saying she hoped they would sleep well.

The sun was shining brightly the next time the children opened their eyes. They took shower baths and then put on their school clothes. As they walked into the dining room a little later, Flossie saw a strange man seated at the table. He was older than Nada's father but looked exactly like him.

"Grandpa!" Nada cried, rushing up to him and hugging him.

"Well, how are you, dear?" Grandpa Bergen said. "And I see you have a visitor."

Nada introduced Flossie, and Grandpa Bergen said he had heard Nada mention the two sets of Bobbsey twins several times.

"You must all come up to Big Bear Pond and visit me sometime," he invited. "I'm sure Nada has told you all about my performing bears. Well, you probably wonder why I happened to come down here so early this morning," he said. "My reason is that I've come to take Hugs home."

Nada and Flossie looked at each other and then hung their heads. Finally Grandpa Bergen's little granddaughter said:

"We think Hugs has been stolen!"

Grandpa Bergen wrinkled his brow and asked when this had happened. Nada told him the sad story. When she finished, he said:

"I guess I can't blame you, if you chained Hugs properly. But this is quite a shock to me.

Hugs was my best performing bear. I have a chance to sell him to a circus at once for a good price."

"Oh, Grandpa, what will we do?" Nada cried.

Mr. Bergen said he did not know. He was having a good bit of bad luck with his bears recently. Two had been ill and were unable to perform. And another one, a favorite of his named Bobo, was missing.

"Did he run away?" Nada asked.

"I thought so until a few minutes ago, but now that I hear Hugs was taken, I begin to wonder whether there is somebody around stealing my bears."

Suddenly Flossie walked up to old Mr. Bergen. "I think Joe and Al took him," she said.

CHAPTER IX

OFFICER O'BRIEN

"WHO are Joe and Al?" Grandpa Bergen asked Flossie.

Flossie said she did not know their last names, but they had a horse van and carried a bear in it.

"Oh yes, Grandpa," Nada spoke up. "We thought Hugs was in the van, but he wasn't. The bear in there looked an awful lot like one of yours, though."

Grandpa Bergen was startled to hear this. He wanted to know where the horse van was. The children could tell him little more about it. But they were sure they would know the men if they should see them again.

"A state trooper saw them, too," Flossie told him, "and so did our Sam."

"Then it should not be too hard to identify the horse van and the men who drove it," Nada's grandfather said.

He left the table and went to the telephone to give the details to the police department. Mrs.

Bergen said the children must eat their breakfast now. She served them orange juice and big bowls of oatmeal. But, as they ate, the little girls continued to talk about the mystery with Grandpa Bergen.

Suddenly a look of delight came over Flossie's face. She said if the same men had stolen Hugs, this would prove it was not the bear that had hurt Freddie.

"That's right," said Nada. "So when Hugs is found, he won't have to go to jail."

As soon as the children finished eating, they said good-by to Grandpa Bergen and Nada's parents. Flossie thanked them very much for her nice visit and said she would pick up her suitcase on the way home from school.

On the way, the girls met Bert and Nan. Nan said Freddie was feeling much better and she was planning a little entertainment for him that afternoon.

"Each of us is going to put on a little show," she told Flossie. "You be thinking about what you will do."

It was nearly noontime before Flossie decided. Then she thought it would be fun to have "living pictures" with the Bobbseys' pets. Besides Snap and Waggo, they had a cat named Snoop.

The day seemed to drag for the Bobbsey twins. Nothing particularly exciting happened at school, and it was not until the last bell rang and they started for home, that the quiet of the day was broken.

Bert and Charlie Mason left the school building together. Very soon they realized that Danny Rugg was following them. The boys were surprised at this because they knew he was supposed to stay after school and help Mr. Tetlow.

Danny drew closer to them as they went past the playground. Suddenly it occurred to Bert that Danny was going to start a fight the instant he got beyond the school grounds.

"I'm not going to give him a chance!" Bert Bobbsey told himself.

More to tease Danny than because he was afraid of having a fight, Bert took hold of Charlie's arm, turned him around unexpectedly and hurried him over to the playground. Then he turned back and started grinning at Danny.

"I thought you had to work after school," he said.

"I do, but I'm going to get square with you first," Danny threatened.

"Get square with me for what?" Bert asked innocently.

"For telling Mr. Tetlow a lot of lies about me!" Danny stormed. "I dare you to come off the school playground and fight fair."

"Danny, you're crazy," said Bert. "I didn't tell Mr. Tetlow anything. I took my punishment and worked. You'd better keep out of any more trouble and not start a fight. I'm going to stay right here until you go back into the building."

Charlie was disgusted. "Why should you worry about Danny, Bert?" he said. "Anyhow, you could lick him any day."

"Is that so?" Danny sneered. "Come out here and I'll show you."

Bert was dying to give Danny a good licking, but he knew Danny was on the verge of being expelled. One more infringement of the rules and he might have to leave school! He did not bother to explain this, however, and finally Danny became worried that his punishment might be made even worse than it already was. He moved off finally, muttering:

"I'll get even with you, you old sissy!"

Charlie was so angry by this time that he started for Danny. But Bert raced after him and held his friend back. He now told him his worry that Danny might be expelled and Charlie stopped.

By the time Bert reached home, his two sisters were busy planning the show for Freddie. Flossie was out in the kennel brushing Snap and Waggo. She was having a hard time with the fox terrier, because he thought this was a nice game and tried to grab the wire brush away from her. But finally the dogs' coats glistened and she took her pets in the house. Snoop was already there, curled up in her basket in a corner of the dining room. The little girl carried Snoop upstairs and told the dogs to follow. Freddie was sitting up in bed with a couple of pillows behind him. Mrs. Bobbsey was seated in a chair beside him, and Dinah stood in the doorway. Nan explained that they were the audience.

The first number on the program was a duet by Nan and Bert. They had just learned the song in school that day, and it was a humorous one about a frog and an old lady. Nan was the old lady and Bert the frog. Freddie laughed loudly as Bert played his part, croaking and hopping around the old woman.

Next, Bert did some sleight-of-hand tricks at which he was very good. Freddie tried his best to guess how his brother did them, but he could not figure it out. He was very happy when Bert finally consented to show him one of the simple tricks.

In the meantime, Nan had left the room. She returned wearing a suit of her father's which dragged on the floor and came down over her hands. She began to recite nursery rhymes in a funny voice and every once in a while she would stop and make a funny remark. Freddie never stopped laughing, but he fairly howled with delight when Nan said:

"Mary had a little lamb
You've heard that tale before,

But have you heard she passed her plate
And had a little more?"

When Nan's act ended, Flossie asked Bert and
Nan to hold up a sheet as a curtain for her stage.
Behind this, the little girl arranged her pets one
on top of the other like a pyramid. When Bert
and Nan pulled the curtain aside, Freddie
laughed with delight.

Dinah and Mrs. Bobbsey went to the attic for
costumes to wear in their act. Just then Nan
happened to glance out the window and cried:

"A policeman's coming to our house!"

The entertainment for Freddie ended at once.
Bert, Nan, and Flossie hurried down the

front stairway with the dogs racing after them.

Just as they reached the first floor, the policeman rang the bell. Bert opened the door and the policeman stepped into the hall. Looking at the boy, he said:

"Are you Bert Bobbsey?"

"Yes, sir," Bert replied.

"I'm Officer O'Brien," the policeman introduced himself. Then, looking at the other children, he said, "Bert, I'd like to talk to you alone."

CHAPTER X

BERT'S CLUE

"YOU want to see me alone?" Bert Bobbsey asked the policeman.

The boy was worried. He could not think of anything he had done to make the police want to talk to him. Was it possible it had something to do with school?

"I—I guess we can go into my father's study," said Bert.

Whatever the policeman wanted to say, he evidently did not want Nan and Flossie to hear it.

Officer O'Brien followed Bert into the study and closed the door himself.

Outside, Nan and Flossie looked at each other, then Nan beckoned her small sister to come away. She herself called Snap and Waggo and said she would put them back in the kennel.

Flossie went as far as the kitchen. There she stopped and stood lost in thought. She was dreadfully worried about what was going to happen to Bert. Why was it such a big secret?

The more she thought about the whole thing, the more Flossie wanted to know what was going on. She knew that eavesdropping was not right. But Bert was her own brother. Why couldn't she know what the trouble was?

Looking out a window, she saw Nan open the kennel door and shoo the dogs inside. Then Nan herself went in. Flossie saw her pick up the dogs' dishes, evidently to clean them. This would take some time.

Flossie thought maybe she should go upstairs and tell her mother what was happening. But this would take time and she might miss something. Flossie could not resist the temptation to tiptoe back to the study.

The little girl put her ear to the crack of the door and listened. At first there was only a murmur of voices, but suddenly she could hear Officer O'Brien very clearly.

"Bert," he said, "the police have been making a thorough investigation of the place where Freddie had his accident. We have come to the conclusion that it was not the missing bear which caused Freddie to be thrown off his bike. Someone riding a bicycle hit your small brother."

"Yes, sir?" was all Bert said.

The policeman went on to say that the person who had caused the accident and had not waited to help Freddie, had evidently come back later to cover up his tracks.

"Yes, I know that," said Bert.

Officer O'Brien chuckled. "That's exactly what I thought you'd own up to."

"What do you mean?" Bert asked him.

"Now, son, take it easy," the policeman said.

Flossie wondered what in the world the officer meant. He did not explain but went on to say that the rider of the bicycle evidently had tried to swerve out of the way but had not been able to. The headlight had hit Freddie on the back of the head. Probably the mysterious rider had lost his balance. He and his bike had tumbled to the ground and the headlight had been smashed.

"We found several bits of the glass," said Officer O'Brien. "We took them to the bicycle shop downtown and the man identified them at once."

"You mean, he knew what bike they came from?" Bert questioned.

"Yes, he did, and, Bert Bobbsey, the bicycle that hit Freddie was yours!"

"Oh!" Bert cried. "The bike was stolen from me."

The policeman cleared his throat before he spoke again. Then he said:

"Bert, you probably have been wondering why I wanted to talk to you alone. The reason is that I'm giving you a chance to confess."

"What do you mean?" Bert asked him.

Officer O'Brien did not answer the question. Instead he said, "Bert, where were you at six o'clock the night of the accident?"

"At six o'clock? Why—I—was on my way home from Charlie Mason's."

"Can you prove that you were not alone?" the policeman asked.

"But I was alone," Bert said. In fact, he went on to say, there had been no one on the street as he walked along. But what did this have to do with his stolen bike?

"Bert," Officer O'Brien said rather severely, "I'm giving you a chance to confess. No one can prove that it wasn't you who was riding the bike that hit your little brother. I suppose you felt pretty bad about it and were trying to cover up. But the whole thing is very ugly. The best thing for you to do is to make a full confession to your family."

Outside the door, Flossie Bobbsey held her breath. This was a dreadful situation! She was sure her older brother would never have done such a thing. Before she thought twice, the little girl opened the door and rushed into the study. She ran over to the policeman and grabbed his coat in her two fists. She tried to shake him.

"You're a bad policeman!" she said angrily. "My brother Bert is the best brother in the world.

He wouldn't hurt anybody and he's a good bike rider, too. He wouldn't run into anybody. You musn't say he hurt Freddie. He didn't!"

Officer O'Brien was extremely surprised. He took Flossie's hands from his coat and looked at her.

"So you've been listening," he said. "Well, I've given your brother a chance to explain, but he doesn't seem to want to. Perhaps we had better call in the rest of the family now."

"I'll get Mother," Flossie offered and hurried from the room.

In a few moments Mrs. Bobbsey came downstairs and heard the story. At the end she said:

"Officer O'Brien, if my son says his bicycle was stolen and that he was not riding it at the time of Freddie's accident, I believe him."

The policeman looked a little uncomfortable. He admitted that perhaps he had been too harsh with Bert.

"If your bike was stolen, why didn't you report it to the police?" he asked.

"I didn't think of doing it," Bert admitted. "I was trying to find it myself."

Suddenly Mrs. Bobbsey asked the officer why he had been so sure of his case. Just because Bert's bicycle had been identified as the one in the accident, this was not proof that her son had hit Freddie.

The policeman said that a telephone call had come to headquarters, accusing Bert of causing Freddie's accident.

"Who was it?" Bert asked angrily.

The officer had to admit that the person had not left his name. While the police did not ordinarily pay too much attention to anonymous messages, in this case the two things seemed to go together—the identification of the bicycle and the telephone call.

"I'm sorry if I was hard on you, Bert," the policeman said. "Even the police department can make mistakes sometimes."

He left the house and the Bobbsey family discussed his accusation for some time. Bert said he wondered if Danny had called headquarters and tried to play a joke on Bert.

"I think it's more likely," said Mrs. Bobbsey, "that it was the person who stole your bicycle. He was trying to shift the blame from himself."

Bert guessed that it might have been Biff Rand, but he kept this to himself. Walking out into the hall, he picked up the local telephone book. Opening it to the page where the R's were, he ran his finger down until he came to the name Rand. There were three listed in Lakeport.

Bert dialed the first one and, when a woman answered, asked if anyone by the name of Biff lived there. She said no and Bert hung up. He tried the next number with the same result.

"I wonder what luck I'll have this time," Bert said to himself as he dialed the third number.

A man's voice answered the telephone. When Bert asked if he had the right number for a person named Biff Rand, the man said no, but he added:

"That's funny you should have asked me this. Someone called up just a short time ago and asked me the same question."

"Do you know who called?" Bert asked, thinking he might pick up a clue.

Mr. Rand said police headquarters had called, and that the captain had told him Biff Rand was wanted by the police.

Bert was not too surprised to hear this, but he asked, "Do you know why he is wanted, Mr. Rand?"

"Yes. He's accused of stealing."

CHAPTER XI

NAN'S SEARCH

"IT'S too bad about this Biff Rand," said the Mr. Rand to whom Bert was talking on the telephone. "I wonder how much is his own fault. I understand from the police that he has been helping some men steal. Probably they put Biff up to it."

Bert began to wonder whether the same men who had the bear had put Biff up to stealing Bert's bicycle. To Mr. Rand, he said, "Do you know anything about Biff, sir?"

Mr. Rand said no. He added that he was sorry anyone with his name should be a thief. He hoped Biff and the men he was with would soon be caught.

Bert put down the telephone and sat lost in thought. Nan came through the hall and said:

"A penny for your thoughts."

Her twin told her what he had learned. With men involved in the theft of Bert's bicycle, there was little chance of his getting it back.

"If those men had anything to do with stealing the bicycle," said Nan, "they didn't have it in the horse van when they were taking the bear away."

"But you said Biff wasn't with them at the time," Bert argued, "so he might have been stealing my bike and taking Hugs just about then. Maybe he planned to meet the men later."

His twin sighed. "It's an awful mixup all right. I wish I could help you and Nada straighten everything out."

That night Nan lay in bed a long time before she went to sleep. She was determined to help Bert get his bicycle back. At the moment she could think of no way to do this, but when she awoke in the morning she had an answer.

"I'll do my detective work in secret," she told herself, smiling. "Oh, I hope it works!"

Before leaving for school, Nan sat down at her desk and printed a sign. It read:

IF ANYONE HAS BOUGHT A BICYCLE
IN THE PAST THREE DAYS, PLEASE
LET NAN BOBBSEY KNOW, ROOM 27.

Nan started for school ahead of Bert and Flossie. She hurried to Mr. Tetlow's office and asked permission to put the sign on the bulletin board.

"Just tell me your reason, Nan, and I'll give you permission," the principal replied.

"Bert's bicycle was stolen from school," Nan

explained. "I think maybe the person who took it painted it and sold it. I thought this would be a good way to find out."

Mr. Tetlow said he thought it was an excellent idea. He told her to post the notice at once. Though practically all the people in the school passed the bulletin board sometime during the day, no one sent a message to Nan Bobbsey. As she looked at the clock nearing closing time, Nan felt very disappointed. Her plan had failed!

"Maybe I can put a notice on the town bulletin board," she told herself.

As soon as school was over, Nan took down her notice and went to the police station. She walked into Captain Roscoe's office and made the same request as she had to Mr. Tetlow. He granted it at once.

"I'm sorry about what happened up at your house when Bert was accused of running into Freddie," he said. "Our Officer O'Brien got a little excited."

Nan said, "Oh, that's all right, but you did give us all a great scare."

"Well, we police have to do our duty, and sometimes it's rather hard on other people," Captain Roscoe said.

Nan left the police station and went at once to the large bulletin board which stood at the edge of the town park. After posting the notice with thumbtacks, Nan crossed out "Room 27" and wrote her address and telephone number on the paper.

While the Bobbsey family was eating supper that evening, the telephone rang. Nan said, "I'll answer it," and jumped up from the table. To her delight, a boy named Arthur Lee was calling to say that he recently had bought a new bicycle. His father had read Nan's notice on the way home from work.

"Do you mind letting me see your bike?" Nan asked.

"No, I don't mind. But why do you want to see it?"

"I'll tell you after I see it," said Nan quietly. "I'll ask my dad to bring me over."

She asked for the boy's address and then went back to the table. Everyone waited for her to tell what the telephone call was about, but Nan said nothing. She still wanted to keep her detective work as a surprise to Bert.

Half an hour later Nan took her father aside and asked him if he would drive her over to Art Lee's house. Mr. Bobbsey said he would be very glad to. When they arrived, they found that Art was a boy around Bert's age who went to a private school. He showed Nan his new bicycle. It was exactly the same shape and make as Bert's but had been painted a different color recently, and all the gadgets Bert had had on it had been removed. There was not even a headlight.

"I hope you won't mind too much," Nan said, "but my brother's very fine bicycle was stolen a few days ago. I have a good idea that the boy who took it, painted it and sold it. Would you mind telling me where you got this bike?"

Art said his father had bought it for him in the near-by town of Westville.

"I sure hope this isn't a stolen bike," Art said, as Nan was leaving. "It sure is a swell bike."

On the way home Nan told her father she had an idea. Nellie Parks had a cousin who lived in Westville and ran a hardware store. He sold new and used bicycles.

"Please let's stop at Nellie's house, Dad, and phone to Mr. Dave Parks," Nan requested.

Her father said he would be glad to. Nellie was excited to hear about Nan's clue and said she would call her cousin at once. Unfortunately, he was not at home and the shop was closed.

"But I know my cousin Dave has the only bicycle store in town," said Nellie, "so Art Lee's father must have bought it there."

"Tomorrow is Saturday," said Nan. "I'm going to ask Mother to drive me over to Westville and talk to your cousin. Could you go, Nellie?"

"Yes, and I'd love to help you solve the mystery," Nellie said excitedly.

The following day Nan and her mother called early for Nellie. It took only half an hour to reach Westville. They went at once to Dave

Parks' store. Nellie's cousin was very busy and they had to wait several minutes before they could speak to him. But finally he came over to them.

He knew Nan, but he had never met Mrs. Bobbsey. As soon as they had been introduced, Nan told him why she had come.

"I remember the boy well who came in to sell me that particular bike which went to Art Lee," said Dave Parks. "He gave me a sad story about his mother being a widow and very ill and he had to have some money right away. Usually I don't buy bicycles before checking up, but this Biff Rand said he was in a great hurry."

So it was Biff Rand! Nan could hardly believe that her plan had been successful.

"Did Biff Rand say where he lives?" she asked the shopkeeper.

"I believe he said it was Rocky Hill," he replied.

Nan thanked Dave Parks for the information, then turned to her mother.

"May we drive to Rocky Hill, please?" she asked.

Her mother smiled and said surely they could not leave the mystery at this point. They left the shop and drove for another half hour. Rocky Hill was a small place and the first person they stopped to speak to told them where the Rands lived.

Mrs. Bobbsey followed the main street to the end and then turned left. She went down to the third house on the right and stopped. She and the girls got out and went to the front door.

Nan's knock was answered by a sweet-faced woman who looked as if she had been crying.

"Are you Mrs. Rand?" Nan asked her.

"Yes, I am. I've never met you before, have I?"

Nan shook her head. Then she asked if Biff Rand lived here. The words were no sooner out of her mouth than Mrs. Rand burst into tears.

"Biff has run away! I don't know where he is!"

CHAPTER XII

AN UNUSUAL ZOO

"YOUR son Biff has run away from home!" cried Nan Bobbsey, shocked.

Her mother and Nellie Parks were sorry to hear this, too. Mrs. Bobbsey asked if the police had been notified.

Mrs. Rand shook her head. "I keep thinking that I'll hear from Biff," she said sadly. "I haven't the least idea where he went."

Suddenly it occurred to her that she had not inquired why the visitors had come. She asked hopefully if they had any news of Biff.

The three callers looked at one another. Mrs. Rand seemed like a very nice person and they hated to tell her that Biff was suspected of being a thief. To ease the situation, Mrs. Bobbsey introduced the three of them to Mrs. Rand. She said they had come because of a mixup which had occurred in Lakeport, and they were eager to talk to Biff about it.

"So my son was in Lakeport?" Mrs. Rand asked eagerly. "Is he still there?"

"We don't know, but we don't think so," Nan replied. "We heard he was traveling with two men named Joe and Al. Do you happen to know who these people are?"

"No, I never heard of them," Mrs. Rand said. "What do they do for a living?"

"We don't know," said Nan, "but they have a horse van."

When Mrs. Rand heard this she said there was no doubt but that her son was with them. All his life Biff had been crazy about horses and other animals, even wild ones. He had always said he would like to join the circus or some wild animal show or a rodeo. She thought perhaps he had left home to find that kind of work.

"I know my son wasn't very happy at home," the boy's mother said. "His father isn't living and we have an awful struggle to get along. It's hard to find work in a little town like this. I do my best and Biff has, too, but we just couldn't seem to get along."

Mrs. Rand tried to smile. "I just know my Biff is planning to earn a lot of money and send it to me."

Again Nan and her mother and Nellie Parks exchanged glances. Here was a totally new slant on the situation! No doubt Biff Rand was a good boy at heart. He had got himself into some kind of trouble, probably because of Joe and Al.

Mrs. Bobbsey smiled understandingly at Mrs. Rand, then she said, "Try not to worry too much. I'm sure Biff will come back before too long."

"Oh, I'm sure he will, too," said Nan enthusiastically. "If we see Biff, we'll tell him you want to hear from him right away."

"Oh, that's wonderful of you," said Mrs. Rand. "Tell my son I won't scold him for running away, because I know he did it to get money for me. But I'd rather have him here with me. We'll get along somehow."

After the callers had left and were driving back to Lakeport, they continued to discuss what they had learned. How they hoped to find Biff quickly and keep him out of any more trouble!

Meanwhile, back in Lakeport, Freddie and Flossie were having a great deal of fun with Susie Larker and Teddy Blake. Freddie was now well enough to be outdoors and play, but Dinah had warned him that he must not do anything strenuous. The four children had talked over what game they would play and had decided upon "zoo." Dinah, overhearing the plans being made on the back porch, had called out:

"Now, Freddie child, don't you go and be no wild animal. If you all want to play zoo, you ought to have a keeper. Freddie, you be the keeper."

This suited Freddie. He instantly decided that this was what he would be when he grew up. The Bobbsey family were always amused at the little boy's ideas of what he wanted to be when he grew up. Every week or so he would decide upon something different. Already he had planned to be a fireman, a policeman, a truck driver, and a detective.

"Wait until I get my key," he said and dashed into the house.

Hanging on a nail near the kitchen door was the key to the gate of the kennel. It was rarely locked, but now Freddie decided that his "animals" should be locked in.

When Freddie came outside, he asked what animals his friends were going to play. Teddy immediately announced that he was going to be a howling wolf.

"I think I'll be a baby bear," said Flossie.

"And I'll be a parrot," said Susie.

Zoo Keeper Freddie shooed his animals toward the kennel, opened the gate, and let them in. At once Snap and Waggo came toward them. Snap walked quietly, but Waggo began to jump all over the children.

"Snap, you're going to be a sleepy old lion," said Flossie, "and, Waggo, you're going to be a wild dog."

Snap lay down in the sunshine at once, as if he understood. Waggo jumped around even more, wagging his stubby tail as if he, too, understood what the game was.

"Now, if you're all ready, let's pretend it's feeding time. I'll get you some grass," said Freddie.

"Grass!" Teddy yelled. "I want cookies."

"Whoever heard of a wolf eating cookies?" Freddie sneered.

With this, he began pulling up handfuls of grass, and tossed them over the fence. Flossie and Susie, giggling, picked up the grass and pretended to eat it, but Teddy still scorned such food. He began to howl like a wolf at the top of his lungs. This started Waggo barking and Snap even got up and bayed with them.

"Caw! Caw! Caw!" screeched Susie.

Flossie was not sure what kind of a noise a baby bear made, but this made no difference because there was already so much noise that she could not have been heard anyway.

As the din kept up, Dinah ran from the kitchen. "Lawsy me!" she cried. "You children have got to be quieter than this. You'll have the fire department up here!"

This remark gave Freddie an idea. "Let's pretend the zoo's on fire!" he yelled.

The little boy dashed into the garage and got out his toy pumper. Freddie was very proud of this piece of fire apparatus. It pumped a fair-size stream of water. Now he turned on the faucet alongside the garage and filled the tank of the engine.

"Here I come!" he cried, and hauled the pumper across the grass to the kennel. Holding up the hose, he aimed it through the fence directly at Teddy, who was still howling.

The little "wolf's" howls ended abruptly and he dashed to the corner of the kennel. Flossie and Susie ran in another direction and Snap and Waggo went into their doghouses. Now Freddie could not reach any of them with the stream of water.

For a moment he stood in disgust, wondering how he could continue the game. "I know what I'll do," he thought. "I'll get the garden hose and turn it on just a little bit."

He let go of the pumper and hurried toward the house. At the moment the hose was attached to a faucet near the kitchen. Freddie turned it on just a wee bit. As soon as he saw the water coming out of the other end of the hose, he picked it up and started for the kennel.

At this moment Danny Rugg came strolling down the driveway. He asked Freddie what game they were playing. After hearing it was zoo, he said this was kid stuff.

"Where's Bert?" he asked.

Freddie said he did not know. Bert had gone out sometime before. "Why do you want him?" Freddie asked.

"To tell him to mind his own business, and if he doesn't, I'm going to fix him!" Danny announced.

Freddie looked alarmed. He asked Danny what Bert had done. "If I tell you, you'll just tell Bert," said Danny, "and that will give him a chance to find an excuse. But he can't get out of it this time!"

Danny steadfastly refused to say any more about it. He suddenly changed the subject and surprised Freddie by saying:

"Hey, I thought you were going to find Hugs."

"We did try," said Freddie.

"Well, you'll never find him," said Danny. "I know where he is."

"You do? Where?" Freddie asked eagerly.

"I don't know whether I should tell you or not," said Danny, "but I guess it won't do any harm. Hugs is on a boat!"

"A boat!" Freddie repeated. "Where?"

Danny wore a triumphant look. He said he would not tell any more about this either.

"Well, I guess I'll go now," he said. "You go on and play your sissy zoo game."

As Danny turned to leave, a car turned into the driveway. Mrs. Bobbsey and Nan were returning home. When they stepped from the car, Freddie started to walk toward them. He had the hose in his hand with a tiny stream of water trickling out. Just before he reached his sister and mother, he suddenly felt the nozzle of the hose give a twist in his hand.

The next instant a huge stream of water shot from the hose and hit Mrs. Bobbsey and Nan directly in the face!

CHAPTER XIII

DANNY LEARNS A LESSON

"OH!" Nan cried, trying to dodge out of the way of the hose.

Mrs. Bobbsey, though she was soaking wet, walked directly into the stream and grabbed the hose from Freddie's hand. The little boy, completely surprised by what had happened, had stood frozen with fear.

"Who turned that hose on full?" Mrs. Bobbsey demanded.

She had seen the small trickle of water and knew that Freddie was not responsible. Suddenly Freddie realized that it must have been Danny Rugg who had played the trick. He told his mother what he suspected.

"That sounds just like Danny!" said Nan indignantly.

Now that Freddie had recovered from his fright, he declared he was going after Danny and turn the hose on him. His mother reminded him that Danny was too far away for this now.

Besides, Freddie was supposed to be resting.

They all heard someone whistling and in a few moments Bert came down the driveway. He looked in amazement at the scene in the Bobbsey back yard, and asked what had happened. Quickly Freddie told him everything, and added: "Why did Danny say you should mind your own business?"

Bert said he had no idea. Danny was always picking a fight with someone. Probably he had made up some crazy story and was trying to make Bert mad.

"And I am mad!" he said. "I'll go right over to Danny and attend to him. He can't soak my sister and mother with the hose and get away with it!"

Bert strode down the driveway and hurried off to Danny Rugg's house. He reached it almost as soon as Danny. The other boy faced him squarely.

"Bert," he said, "what's the big idea of telling it all over town that I stole your bicycle?"

"Hold on, Danny," Bert warned him. "I never told anybody but Charlie Mason that you might have taken my bicycle."

The Bobbsey boy asked Danny to tell him where he had heard the story. When Danny mentioned the soda clerk, a delivery boy, and a newspaper boy, Bert asked:

"Did they say I told them you stole my bike?"

Danny admitted that he had not asked them.

He had just assumed it was Bert. Finally Bert talked the bully into checking the story with the soda clerk. From him they learned that an older boy, a stranger, had told him the story, claiming he had heard it from Bert!

"You see?" Bert said to Danny. "This boy— and I think I know who he is—probably told the delivery boy and the newsboy, too."

Danny had to admit that this was probably the

case. When they left the store, he wanted to know who the boy was whom Bert suspected.

But Bert shook his head. "You're not going to catch me spreading any tales around town. And now suppose you tell me, Danny, how you happen to know that Hugs is on a boat."

Danny said that while he was in the big soda shop, he had overheard two men talking at the next table. One had said, "If we can get the bear to a boat, everything will be okay."

"Of course," Danny continued, "I can't be certain it was Hugs they meant. But I'm pretty sure it must have been."

"Why didn't you tell the police?" Bert asked.

Danny said that he had heard the men talking before Hugs had come to Lakeport. Afterwards, he had not bothered to tell the police, because he was not sure it was Hugs.

"Did you hear what the men's names were?" Bert questioned Danny.

Danny thought a moment, then he said, "I think one called the other Al."

"Then the bear they mentioned could be Hugs!" Bert said excitedly. "We think a man named Al took Hugs."

Bert did not tell Danny any more of the Bobbseys' suspicions. He told him not to turn on the hose again at the Bobbseys', said good-by to the boy, and immediately went to Nada Bergen's house. The little girl and her parents were amazed to hear about this latest clue which Bert had picked up.

"What did Al and Joe mean by taking Hugs on a boat?" the twin asked.

None of the Bergens could figure this out. Mr. Bergen immediately put in a telephone call to his father and asked him. But Grandpa Bergen had no idea either. Finally they all came to the conclusion that Danny must have mistaken the word "boat" for something else. Possibly the man had said truck or van.

"The clue seems to prove one thing," said Nada's father. "Those men deliberately planned to steal Hugs. They must have known my father was going to leave the bear with us. They just waited for a chance to take the bear."

When Bert reached home, the family held a conference. Everyone had something to report, either about the missing Hugs, Bert's bicycle, or the people who were involved in the mystery.

Nan told the story of everything she, Nellie, and Mrs. Bobbsey had learned in Westville and Rocky Hill. Bert was surprised and delighted with his twin's fine detective work. He then told about Danny's accusation and how a boy had started the whispering campaign against Bert.

"I'm sure it was Biff Rand," he said. "He's just trying to cover up his own guilt."

Mr. Bobbsey reported that the police had not found the horse van which had contained the bear they thought was the stolen Bobo. They had traced the fact that the van did not belong to any hunt club or riding academy.

"The van must have been owned by some person who transports horses as a business," Mr. Bobbsey concluded.

He had barely finished speaking when both the front doorbell and the telephone rang. Mrs. Bobbsey laughed, saying this was certainly a busy household.

"I'll go to the front door," said Bert, and Nan said, "I'll answer the telephone."

The caller at the front door proved to be Arthur Lee. He was bringing Bert's bicycle back. Art said he had heard from Dave Parks that the bicycle did belong to Bert. Mr. Parks would return the money Art had paid him.

Bert thanked him and said it was certainly a shame that Dave Parks had to lose all that money. Art replied that the hardware dealer had said the loss was his own fault. He should have checked the boy's ownership before buying the bike.

After Art had left, Bert stood in the hall, listening to his sister's conversation on the telephone. He overheard her say:

"That will be wonderful, Nada. Yes, Mother says we may all go with you to Big Bear Pond tomorrow. We'll pack a lunch, so your grandfather won't have to feed us all," Nan giggled. "You'll pick us up right after church? That's wonderful! Bye now."

Nan looked up at her twin. "I guess you heard most everything," she said. "We're going to spend the day at Big Bear Pond with Mr. and Mrs. Bergen and Nada!"

"That's swell!" Bert cried. He was as enthusiastic as his sister. How exciting it would be to see all the animal tamer's bears!

The following morning Nan and Flossie were up early to help Dinah prepare the picnic lunch which they were to take. Nan buttered bread and Flossie put slices of chicken on them. Dinah filled thermos bottles with hot soup and cold milk. After the sandwiches and drinks had been put into the picnic hamper, the girls selected all kinds of cookies from a batch Dinah had made the day before. Last of all came an ice cream pudding, one of Dinah's special recipes, which Flossie and Freddie declared they liked even better than ice cream.

Later in the morning Mr. and Mrs. Bergen and Nada came to pick up the children in their station wagon. The three girls sat in the center seat with the two boys in the rear.

"How many bears does your grandfather have?" Freddie asked Nada.

The little girl said she did not know exactly.

There were several pens of them. Where the bears were placed depended on what stage of the training they had reached.

"The tamest ones, which are ready to be sold, are nearest the house," Nada said. "They're the ones I like best. Next to Hugs my favorite is Kisses, his twin."

Nada went on to say that Kisses had two babies of her own. They were the cutest cubs one would ever want to see. Their names were Honey and Beesy.

"Oh, I just can't wait to see them!" Flossie exclaimed.

At this moment Freddie pointed out a field in which several beautiful horses were grazing.

"This is horse country," Mr. Bergen stated, and when Freddie wanted to know what this meant, he explained, "Most of the people who live in this section love to ride. They own their own horses and put them in shows and races."

The words were hardly out of his mouth when Mrs. Bergen cried fearfully, "Look out!"

From a side road a horse van careened recklessly across the main highway. Mr. Bergen jammed on his brakes, but it did not seem possible for him to avoid a crash!

CHAPTER XIV

A CLOSE CALL

THE BOBBSEY twins and their friends held their breaths as Mr. Bergen's station wagon and the horse van almost collided. But Nada's father managed to swerve out of the way, his tires screeching. The driver of the van was not so fortunate. His vehicle skidded badly on the pavement and landed with a *whack* against an embankment, turning halfway over.

For a couple of seconds everyone sat in stunned silence. Then Mr. Bergen pulled to the side of the road and got out. The others followed and ran toward the horse van.

They wondered whether the driver would be Joe or Al and whether the missing Bobo would be inside the van. But the driver proved to be a young man. He sat as if dazed, still clutching the wheel and staring straight ahead. When Mr. Bergen spoke to him, he did not reply at once. Finally, however, he turned his head and said:

"I—I guess I was thinking of something else and didn't watch the intersection."

In the meantime Bert and Freddie had gone to the rear of the horse van. Now Bert unlatched it and opened the door. A young pony was lying there on its side. It tried to struggle to its feet but fell back.

"His leg is injured!" Bert cried. "Oh, I hope it's not broken!"

By this time the young man had stepped from the cab and had come around to the back with Mr. Bergen. Upon seeing his injured pony, he began to berate himself again for the accident.

"That pony is worth thousands of dollars!" he said bitterly. "Oh, what am I going to do?"

Nan, very distressed, spoke up, "Can't we take him to a vet right away?"

The young man said he supposed they should. But he did not know how to get him there. He couldn't right the van himself.

"Maybe if we all push," Bert suggested, "we can stand it upright."

The young man, who now introduced himself as Howard Grant, said they could try. Everyone in the group, including the small twins, climbed up the embankment and when Mr. Bergen said, "One, two, three!" they all pushed as hard as they could. The van slowly righted and once more rested on four wheels.

Everyone noticed that Howard Grant was

shaking. He admitted that the accident had been a great shock to him and he did not dare drive to the veterinarian's. Mr. Bergen offered to do this while his wife drove the station wagon.

"Oh, please, may I ride with the pony?" Freddie spoke up.

All the children wanted to, but Mr. Bergen did not think this would be too good for the pony. It was finally decided that Bert and Nada, who had had some experience with horses, would be the ones to ride with the injured animal.

On the way to the veterinarian's, Howard Grant said that his father owned a farm on which he raised horses and ponies. He was delivering the valuable pony to his new owner when the accident occurred.

"Mr. Grant," Bert spoke up—he was talking through the little window between the back of the van and the cab—"did you ever hear of two men who use a horse van to carry bears in?"

Howard Grant smiled and said he had never heard of such a thing. Bert went on to tell him that he knew of two men named Joe and Al who did this.

"We've been trying for several days to find them," said Bert.

Howard Grant looked startled to hear this. "Did you say one of the men's names was Joe?"

When Bert said yes, Mr. Grant added, "I

don't know anything about bears, but a man named Joe Shunter bought an old horse van from my father not long ago. He said he needed it as an extra vehicle for transporting animals for some kind of a show."

"I'll bet he's the one we're looking for!" Bert exclaimed. "Where does he live?"

Unfortunately, Howard did not know. When the group reached Dr. Walter's clinic, the doctor made a brief examination of the pony. Then he went inside the clinic for a rope and a big stretcher.

After tying the pony's fore and hind feet so that he could not kick, Dr. Walter, the two men, and Bert lifted the animal onto the stretcher. This was no easy task, but at last it was done and Bert helped the three men carry the animal inside.

A little later Mr. Bergen and Bert came out to report that the pony would be as good as new in about a month.

"And Howard Grant is feeling better, too," Bert added. "He says he can carry on from here without our help."

The children were delighted to hear this and climbed into the station wagon. Once more they set off for Big Bear Pond and a short time later reached it with no more mishaps.

Grandpa Bergen's estate was in a deep woods on a little-used road far back from the main

They carried the pony on the stretcher

highway. The stone house was large and rambling.

Nada was the first one to jump from the car. She ran up to meet her grandfather, who came out the front door. The twins followed and she introduced them all. Flossie, of course, already knew him.

"Well, I'm certainly glad you all came," he said, smiling.

Quickly Nada and the others told Mr. Bergen what had happened on the road and how they had learned that the man who had probably taken Bobo was named Joe Shunter.

"Well, you young folks are regular detectives," Grandpa Bergen said. "I suppose you'll have this mystery solved before the police can do it!"

The children laughed and said they wished he might be right. But Bert suggested that Grandpa Bergen notify the authorities just the same.

"I'll do that at once," the animal trainer said.

By this time the older people had come up and he kissed his daughter-in-law and shook hands with his son. Mrs. Bergen suggested that the children carry the lunch from the car and take it into the house.

"Would you like to eat at once?" Grandpa Bergen asked. "Or do you want to see the bears first? I thought you'd like to play a game of hide-and-seek with Kisses and her cubs."

CHAPTER XV

A BOXING BEAR

OF COURSE all the Bobbsey twins and Nada Bergen, too, wanted to play hide-and-seek with the bears!

Flossie looked a little afraid and said the others should go first. Freddie was already running toward one of the cages, but Grandpa Bergen told him he must wait until his turn came.

"I believe it would be best if Nada went first and showed you how to play the game," he said.

In a large, fenced-in enclosure some distance away from the house was a large black bear and two beautiful cubs.

"That's Kisses," Nada explained. "Isn't she lovely?"

"She's bee-yoo-ti-ful!" Flossie exclaimed. "Are those her babies, Honey and Beesy?"

Nada nodded. She said Kisses was one of the nicest mother bears her grandfather had ever had. At this remark Flossie looked a little sad. She said:

"If she's so nice, I shouldn't think your grand-father would want to sell her."

Nada smiled. "Most of my grandfather's bears are nice. If he kept them all, he'd have so many he wouldn't know what to do with them."

Grandfather Bergen overheard the remark. He laughed and said, "And I shouldn't have any money to live on either."

He opened the gate to the enclosure and Nada went inside.

"Hello, Kisses," said Nada, going up to the big, black mother bear and stroking her nose gently.

Kisses put up her right paw and shook hands with the little girl. Nada now went to one of the cubs and tried to shake his hand, but the little bear ran away and hid behind a tree. The other cub followed.

For a few minutes the visitors stood and watched the bears play. It was amazing what fine somersaults the babies could turn! Outside the cage Freddie tried to imitate them.

Presently Kisses made a grunting sound and the two cubs came to her side. All three stood on their hind legs and began to box one another. In a few moments the mother bear evidently thought the children had had enough of a les-son and backed away. Honey and Beesy began to box each other.

"Oh, aren't they funny!" Flossie cried out,

clapping her hands to keep time with the jabs each of the cubs made toward the other one.

"Say," said Bert, "they're pretty swell at boxing!"

The others agreed it was amazing, and Nan asked Grandpa Bergen if Kisses had taught her twins everything they knew about the game.

"Oh, no," Grandpa Bergen replied. "Bears are natural boxers. They just need to be taught a few fine points by the older bears."

In a few moments the cubs dropped to the ground and Grandpa Bergen announced that the game was over. He said it was time for Nada to play hide-and-seek with the bears. At once the little girl ran and hid behind a tree.

Kisses waited until Nada peeked from behind the trunk, then she started to run after her. Honey and Beesy looked on for a few moments, then they, too, ran for trees and hid behind them.

Freddie and Flossie were so excited, they jumped up and down in glee.

"Oh, I just can't wait for a turn!" Freddie exclaimed.

"You may be next," Grandpa Bergen told him.

After Nada and the bears had dodged among the trees for several minutes, Nada came to the gate and walked from the enclosure.

"All right, Freddie," said Grandpa Bergen.

The little boy walked inside. It was not until he stood facing the big, black mother bear that Freddie's heart began to thump wildly. He hoped she was as tame as the others had told him she was.

"You start the game," Grandpa Bergen called out.

Freddie hurried across the enclosure and hid behind the tree Nada had chosen. At once Kisses started lumbering toward him.

"I wonder why she's picking on me," the little boy thought as he saw Honey and Beesy also dodge behind trees. Their mother did not go toward them.

Before Kisses reached him, Freddie dodged around the tree, ran across the enclosure, and hid behind another big trunk. Kisses growled a little and turned around. She hurried toward the little boy. When she had reached the tree, Freddie again came from in back of it, dashed past her, and hid behind a tree on the opposite side. This was fun!

Once more Freddie tried this way of playing the game, but he misjudged the distance. As he hurried past the bear, Kisses turned quickly, made a leap toward him, and cuffed him hard on the side of the head. Freddie tumbled over!

Quickly the little boy got up and tried to run again. But once more Kisses lifted her right paw and smacked him on the cheek. Now Freddie was frightened and he looked toward the gate for help from the Bergens. But Grandpa Bergen and Nada stood there laughing loudly.

"They don't care at all what happens to me," thought Freddie in panic.

He was just trying to figure out what to do, when Grandpa Bergen called out, "Kisses doesn't think you're playing the game fairly. When her cubs don't behave, she always cuffs them."

Freddie was surprised to hear this. He had thought he was pretty smart, dodging from tree to tree. Sheepishly he asked:

"What did I do wrong?"

"Kisses expects you to stay there until she tags you," Nada explained.

"All right," said Freddie.

Meekly he hurried toward one of the big trees and hid behind the trunk. This time he stood still and Kisses came over. She merely tapped his arm. Freddie felt better. As soon as Kisses left to go tap her cubs, who had moved from their original hiding places, Freddie walked over to the gate.

Flossie still felt a bit timid about playing hide-and-seek with the bears. The little girl thought she would skip the game. Nan went inside and had lots of fun. She even got the mother bear to hide and went to find her. When Nan's turn ended, Bert walked in, and for a few minutes the game proceeded as it had with the others. Then Bert asked Grandpa Bergen if he might box with the bears.

"Well, you can try," was the reply. "No one has ever boxed with them before."

Bert had a little trouble making Kisses understand, but at last the mother bear stood on her hind legs and gently boxed with the boy. Then Honey, the cub, tried the game, but Bert had to keep dodging to avoid her slaps which were not nearly so gentle as her mother's!

Then Beesy, too, enjoyed a tussle with Bert. Finally the cub dropped to the ground and began to do a series of somersaults. Honey and Kisses got down and rolled and somersaulted too.

"Maybe I should play that game," Bert laughed. He got down and rolled, somersaulted, and romped with the three bears.

"Oh, Bert's wonderful!" cried Flossie. "He ought to be in the animal show with the bears."

The entertainment was suddenly interrupted by a loud continuous blasting of an automobile horn. Apparently Grandpa Bergen had more visitors. Kisses gave a whoof of rage, as if she did not like the game to be interrupted.

Bert got up and started toward the gate. Honey and Beesy had run off, but their mother apparently did not intend that the boy should leave. She hurried toward Bert and began to shove him with her two front paws.

"Hey, what's the big idea?" Bert cried out.

Kisses refused to let him go to the gate. Each time he tried it, she got in front of him and booted him in the opposite direction. Finally the mother bear put her two forelegs around the boy's neck and shoved him toward one of the trees.

Bert could not understand why. He had thought she was his friend. Dodging, he tried to escape Kisses. With that, she gave him a resounding whack!

CHAPTER XVI

AN AMAZING DISCOVERY

"CLIMB a tree, Bert!" Grandpa Bergen ordered.

Hearing this, Bert Bobbsey shinned up the nearest tree as fast as he could. As soon as he was a few feet up the trunk, Kisses gave a grunt of satisfaction and walked off. She lumbered toward the fence, giving woofs of anger now and then.

Bert noticed that both Honey and Beesy were up in a tree not far from him. They were clinging tightly and looking toward their mother.

Nada called out, "Whenever there's danger, a mother bear always makes her cubs go up a tree."

Bert laughed. Did Kisses think he was one of her cubs? Anyway, he was glad of her protection. She could win a fight much easier than he could.

"She likes Bert," Flossie spoke up proudly.

As Kisses continued to sniff the air and give little grunts of displeasure, the others wondered who had come in the car. There was no doubt but that the honking of the horn had disturbed the mother bear.

"I'm afraid you'll have to stay up in that tree until I find out who's here," Grandpa Bergan called to Bert.

He hurried off toward his house. The others tried to guess who had arrived.

"You don't suppose it could be that bad Joe and Al?" Flossie asked fearfully.

Mrs. Bergen said she was sure they would not dare come there. Nevertheless, Nada, Nan, and Flossie hurried off to the house to find out. Coming toward them was Grandpa Bergen and two strange men. As they reached the children, Mr. Bergen said:

"Our callers are interested in buying Kisses."

All the girls felt bad to hear this. The bear and her cubs were so appealing that it seemed sad for them to be separated.

"I just can't bear to see Kisses taken away," said Flossie. "Let's take a walk and see some other bears."

This was agreeable to Nada, who led the two girls deeper into the woods. They paused for a few minutes to see several black bears which Nada said were in training.

"I'll see if I can make them do any tricks,"

she told the others. The bears were lying down, and though Nada coaxed them over and over, they refused to get up. Finally she said it was too bad the children had brought nothing for the bears to eat—that would make them come to the fence.

"This is the wrong time of year for acorns," the little girl said, looking around. "You know bears love acorns and sweet leaves."

Flossie said perhaps she could find sweet leaves, and looked all around. But though Nan and Nada helped her, the girls could not find any leaves sweet enough to suit the bears.

Finally the girls gave up and walked several hundred feet to another cage. These bears were no more sociable than the others, and in disappointment Nada started to turn back.

"I know a shortcut to the house," she said. "There's a lane over here. Come on!"

She led Nan and Flossie a little distance to the right. In a few moments they came out on the dirt road. As she started along it, Nan heard a noise behind her. Facing about, she was just in time to see a deer lope across the road.

And Nan saw something else, too—something very exciting! A horse van was parked at the side of the lane! She called Nada's and Flossie's attention to it and then started to run toward it. The other girls followed.

"Nada, does this belong to your grandfather?" Nan asked.

"No, I'm sure it doesn't."

"Then what is it doing here?" the older Bobbsey twin asked.

Nada said she did not know. It certainly seemed like a funny place for a horse van to be parked. No one was in the driver's seat, but she suggested that someone might be inside.

"And maybe there's a horse or a pony in it," Flossie suggested. "Let's see."

The three girls hurried to the rear of the van. The doors were wide open, but there was nothing inside. Suddenly Nan gave a cry.

"Nada! Flossie! Do you know what I think? I think that is Joe and Al's van!"

"You do?" Nada asked. She was beginning to be frightened.

Nan pointed to the padding on the left side of the van. It had a long rip exactly like one she had noticed in the van which had been carrying the bear.

The instant Nan made her announcement, the three girls had the same idea. Was it possible that Joe and Al had come to steal a bear from Grandpa Bergen?

"We must stop them!" Nan cried.

"But how could we?" Nada asked. "They are big strong men."

Nan said she knew this. They could not hope to stop the men by physical force. But perhaps they could get help.

"Let's go back to your grandfather's house as fast as we can," she suggested.

"We'll take the shortcut," Nada said.

The three girls set off with Nada leading the way. They ran, stumbled, and turned their ankles several times over hard ground.

Flossie was getting farther and farther behind. Suddenly she fell headlong over a tree root and screamed. Nan hurried back to her.

"Oh, my foot!" Flossie cried.

Nan examined it and thought Flossie had bruised it on a stone. She called for Nada to come back, and together the two carried Flossie the rest of the way.

Considerable time was consumed because the going was slow now. Eventually they reached Grandpa Bergen's home. No one was in sight.

"Those men have gone," Nan said, pointing to where the car had stood.

Nada said she thought her grandfather must have joined the others at different cages. She would go and find out. When she did not return, Nan became fidgety.

"Does your foot feel better? Do you think you can walk on it now?" she asked Flossie.

The small twin tried it out. "It hardly hurts at all," she said.

"Then let's go after Nada," said Nan. "The men who came in the horse van may take it away before we get there."

The two Bobbsey girls hurried along the trail which Nada had taken. They went past Kisses' cage. No one was there. They hurried along to the next two, where the bears were not so friendly. No one was in sight.

"We'd better call," Nan suggested.

She and Flossie yelled at the top of their lungs. For several seconds there was no response. Then from far away came an answering hello.

"They are way over this way," said Nan, starting off through the deep woods.

She took Flossie's hand and they went fairly slowly so that the little girl would not fall again. In a few minutes the two groups met. Nada had just reached them, too, from another direction, and had begun to tell the story of the horse van to her grandfather.

"I don't like the sound of this at all," he said, a frown creasing his forehead. "We'll look into it at once!"

He strode off among the trees. Mr. and Mrs. Bergen and the children followed quickly.

"Oh, I hope those bad men didn't take another bear!" cried Flossie, who blamed herself for the delay.

Grandpa Bergen called back that he did not think the men would try to steal a bear until nighttime, when the darkness would hide their actions.

"Let's hope they haven't somehow been warned and driven off," he said. "I want to find out exactly who they are and what they're up to!"

CHAPTER XVII

A WONDERFUL INVITATION

IN A few minutes the Bobbseys and the Bergens reached the lane.

"Which way do we go now to find the horse van?" Grandpa Bergen asked the girls.

"Up this way," Nada answered.

"Oh, I don't think so," said Nan. "I'm sure it was down there."

Flossie admitted she did not have the least idea where they had seen the van. It was finally decided to go toward the main road. If they did not come to it, then they would turn back and look in the other direction. As they hurried along, the girls kept looking for landmarks which they might recognize. Presently Nan cried out:

"Isn't this the place where we went into the woods, Nada?"

"Yes, I think it is."

Bert and Freddie stopped to examine the spot and declared they could see footprints turning into the woods. The searchers hurried on. But they did not see the van. Nan ran up alongside Nada and said:

"We didn't come this far the first time we saw the van, did we?"

"I don't think so," said Nada, "but we could be wrong."

Bert had outdistanced the others. Suddenly he called back:

"I see tracks in the road."

The others hurried to where the Bobbsey twin stood. Tire marks were plainly visible in the dirt lane. But there was no sign of the horse van.

"Oh dear, they got away!" Nada cried in disappointment.

Her father, upon examining the tracks, declared that actually there were two sets. The horse van must have backed out in practically the same tracks it had made when it had entered the lane.

"The driver must have been in the woods and heard you girls talking," he said. "It didn't take him long to leave."

While Mr. Bergen was speaking, Bert had been looking at something else in the road—two sets of a man's footprints. One came into the lane, the other went out. He called the attention of his companions to them.

"Maybe the man wasn't in the woods, Mr. Bergen," he suggested. "He may have walked in from the main highway."

The others looked at the footprints and agreed that Bert had a good idea. Probably after the driver had parked the van, he had walked out to the highway to join someone else. Later he had walked back.

"Well, however it was," said Grandpa Bergen, "I'm glad the van is gone."

"Are you sure the driver didn't take one of your bears?" his son asked him.

"I can't be sure, of course, until I count my bears," he said. "But I don't believe there was enough time to do it."

He turned to Nan, Nada, and Flossie and smiled. "I think I have you girls to thank for saving me from the loss of a bear."

Mrs. Bergen suggested that they walk to the end of the lane to be sure the horse van was not parked on the highway.

"All right, suppose some of you do that," said Grandpa Bergen. "I feel that I must get back to the house and the bears, and protect them."

"Suppose we divide forces," his daughter-in-law said. "Who wants to go back with Grandpa and who wants to go up to the highway?"

Bert, Nada, Nan, and Flossie chose to go with Grandpa Bergen. The others would take the highway.

When Freddie's group reached the end of the road and did not see the horse van, the little boy thought a moment, then said:

"Why don't we build a stone road block in the middle of the lane? Then nobody can drive in or out without moving the stones. Those bad men won't want to take time to do that."

"Good idea, Freddie!" Mr. Bergen said.

They found an old tumbledown stone wall and began to take it apart. Mr. Bergen lifted the heavy stones and Mrs. Bergen and Freddie carried the smaller ones. Soon they had a blockade!

"We ought to make it real strong like the soldiers do," said Freddie.

"What do you suggest?" Mr. Bergen asked him.

Freddie said he thought they should shovel a lot of sand and soil all down among the stones and then lay tree limbs over the pile. He giggled.

"Maybe we can find something real scratchy," he said. "Like blackberry bushes."

Mr. and Mrs. Bergen laughed merrily. They thought all this was a great deal of work, but they were willing to carry it through. Mr. Bergen hunted around for something he could use for a shovel, while his wife searched the roadside for berry bushes with prickles on them. She was more successful than her husband, and in the end all three of the roadblock builders figured that the thorny bushes would be enough to discourage anyone.

Mr. Bergen dug them out with the end of a fallen fence post, and the three of them dragged the bushes by the roots up to the pile of stones. When they were heaped over it, Mrs. Bergen said they really must hurry back to the cottage.

Meanwhile, Bert had been offering a plan of his own to Grandpa Bergen to keep burglars away.

"Why don't you rig up an alarm system, sir?" he suggested.

"I never thought of that," Nada's grandfather

replied. "As a matter of fact, I never had any bears taken until recently. You know, not just anyone would steal a bear. It would have to be someone familiar with their habits, or a person who had worked with them."

Bert was surprised to hear this. At once he realized that the men who had stolen Bobo and perhaps Hugs must be experts at handling animals. This ought to narrow the search in finding them.

"Now this alarm system you mentioned, Bert," said Grandpa Bergen. "How about you helping me rig one up?"

"I'd be very glad to, sir," said Bert. "You mean an electrical system?"

Grandpa Bergen nodded, then his eyes twinkled. "You children have a spring vacation coming up pretty soon, don't you?" he asked.

"Yes, we do," Bert replied. "It starts next Wednesday."

"Then how about the Bobbsey twins and my granddaughter Nada coming to spend a few days with me at Big Bear Pond?" Grandpa Bergen invited. "Then you can help me rig up this alarm system, Bert."

For a second the children merely stared, then they burst into excited chatter and laughter. What a wonderful invitation!

"We'd love to come," Nan spoke up first. "I'm

sure our parents would let us. You don't think we'd be too much trouble?"

"Of course not," said Grandpa Bergen. "There's only one thing that bothers me, though. I'm really not much of a cook. I guess some grownup should come along and keep you children well fed."

Flossie ran up to Grandpa Bergen and took hold of his hand. "Would you like Dinah to come? She's the best cook in Lakeport."

Nan quickly explained who Dinah was and said perhaps her mother would let Dinah cook for Grandpa Bergen during their stay.

"Well, that sounds just perfect," the elderly man smiled. "To tell you the truth, I don't bother too much for myself, and some good cooking would certainly taste good to me."

When Mr. and Mrs. Bergen and Freddie arrived, they were told about the invitation. At once Freddie yelled:

"Yippee! Yippee!"

Everyone laughed at Freddie's exuberance but the others felt just as happy about the vacation at Big Bear Pond as he did. At once Nada began to plan excitedly what they would do while staying with her grandfather.

"Some morning I'll take you to the cave." she said. "It's kind of spooky, but you'll love it."

CHAPTER XVIII

LITTLE DETECTIVES

AS SOON as the Bobbsey twins reached their home in Lakeport, Flossie and Freddie dashed to the kitchen to speak to Dinah.

"How would you like to go and live with bears?" Flossie asked her excitedly.

"Lawsy me, whatever are you talking about?" the cook asked, her eyes growing larger by the moment.

"Oh, the bears are in cages. They won't hurt you," Freddie added.

"Listen here, honey children," said Dinah. "I don't want to go live with any bears. It's right nice here and I'm satisfied."

Suddenly Freddie and Flossie began to giggle. They realized they had not asked Dinah what they had intended to at all. By this time Bert and Nan had also come into the kitchen.

"Nan," said Flossie, "please tell Dinah about going to live where the bears are."

Nan did this, and after Dinah had heard she was going as a cook and did not actually have to live with the bears, she began to laugh. Whenever the jolly cook laughed, she would shake all over and Flossie and Freddie sometimes teased her and said she shook the way Santa Claus did when he laughed.

Then suddenly Dinah became serious. "I won't have to cook for the bears, too, will I?" she asked.

Now it was the twins' turn to laugh. They assured her she would have to cook only for Grandpa Bergen, Nada, and the twins.

Dinah reminded the children that first of all they would have to get their parents' permission to go. If they received this, she would figure out everything about the food, so Mrs. Bobbsey would not have to bother.

The four children were told that their parents had gone to call on friends. They watched eagerly from the front windows for Mr. and Mrs. Bobbsey's return. The minute they saw them coming up the street, the twins hurried from the house to make their request.

"Well, as long as Dinah's willing to go," said Mrs. Bobbsey, "it won't be so much work for Grandpa Bergen. I'll give my consent. What do you think, Dick?"

The twins' father thought it would be a nice trip, but he warned them that they would have to do exactly what Grandpa Bergen requested.

"I don't want you to get into any trouble with those bears," he added meaningfully.

The twins promised to behave perfectly and not break any rules of Grandpa Bergen's bear reserve.

It was hard for the four children to keep their minds on their studies the following day. But finally classes were over and they hurried home.

Bert was the first one home and as he walked into the kitchen, Dinah said:

"You know, a funny thing happened this afternoon. A strange boy came here selling magazines."

"Why is that funny?" Bert asked her.

Dinah said that was not what had bothered her. The boy had seemed very nice and she had bought a magazine from him at the back door.

"He sniffed my baking," the cook went on, "and looked so thin and kind of hungry that I asked him if he would like something to eat. When he said he would, I fixed him a couple of sandwiches and a glass of milk."

Bert did not think this was unusual. Dinah was kind, and proud of her cooking as well. She was always glad to give people a taste of it.

"The boy seemed to like the food, and I didn't pay much attention to him," Dinah went on. "I was busy fixin' some fricassee chicken for dinner.

Then all of a sudden I looked around and he was gone!

"Maybe I wouldn't have thought anything about it," Dinah went on, "except I heard a noise in the garage. So out I went to see what it was. Well, that was when I thought things were funny. That boy was looking over your bicycle, Bert. I thought he seemed entirely too interested, and rememberin' how it had been stolen once, I said to him, 'What you doin', boy?' "

"What did he say?" Bert asked quickly.

"He didn't say nothin'," Dinah replied. "He ran away as fast as he could."

At once Bert asked what the boy looked like. Hearing the description, he was sure the caller had been Biff Rand. Had he planned to steal the bicycle a second time?

At this moment Freddie and Flossie came into the kitchen. Dinah had to tell the story all over again. The twins were excited and when they went out into the back yard to play, Freddie said to his twin:

"Why don't we try to find that bad boy?"

"But how?" Flossie questioned.

Freddie could not answer this. Instead, he suggested they go into the house and talk to Dinah themselves about the boy. Maybe she could give them another clue.

Walking inside, the twins saw Nan looking at a magazine. They learned it was the one which Dinah had bought from the strange boy. The small twins were just in time to hear their sister say:

"Dinah, this magazine must have been stolen by that boy who sold it to you. There's a name and address on it. I'm going to phone these people and find out."

Flossie and Freddie listened intently as Nan called a Mrs. Zigg, who lived on the other side of Lakeport. The woman told Nan that they did receive their magazines by mail, and that this one must have been taken either from their front porch or from the mailman's bag.

Freddie turned to his twin. "If that bad boy took the magazine and sold it, I'll bet he took lots more. Come on, Flossie, I know what to do."

The two children left the house, and Freddie explained his plan. He said they would ring every doorbell on their block and ask if people had bought magazines from a boy. If they had, maybe they could tell the twins something about him.

There were so many houses to go to that the twins divided the work. Flossie took the left side of the street and Freddie the right. Freddie had no luck at all. Several people had bought magazines, but knew nothing about the boy. Flossie had no better luck until she came to the last house. This was where one of her playmates, Sally Smith, lived. Mrs. Smith said that she had heard the boy with the magazines say that he was going to join an animal show.

"Then it'll be easy to find him," said Flossie eagerly.

She hurried across the street to tell Freddie, and the twins ran home. Breathlessly they told their clue to Nan and Bert.

Bert went to the telephone and called their friend Captain Roscoe in the police department. When he asked if there was to be any animal show in the vicinity, the police captain said that one was coming that day to the town of Greensburg. Bert thanked him and hung up.

"Greensburg isn't very far from here," he told the others excitedly. "Maybe we can get somebody to drive us over."

Mrs. Bobbsey was not at home, so Bert telephoned to his dad at the lumberyard. Mr. Bobbsey said that Sam had just come in from a trip and he would excuse him for the balance of the afternoon. He could take Mr. Bobbsey's car and drive Bert and Nan to the animal show.

"I think Freddie and Flossie had better stay at home," Mr. Bobbsey said. "I heard their mother say she had something for them to do as soon as she returned."

The small twins were disappointed not to be included in the trip, but perhaps Mrs. Bobbsey would take them somewhere exciting!

In fifteen minutes Sam picked up Nan and

Bert, and they set off. Sam said he was glad to play detective but wondered what to do with the boy if they should catch him.

"Turn him over to the police," said Bert.

Nan did not comment, but she was bothered by the thought of Biff's being a thief.

When they reached Greensburg Sam inquired the way to the animal show.

What excitement they found upon reaching the place! There were cages and cages of wild

animals. Workmen were rushing about, feeding the animals.

Nan and Bert began to feel discouraged as they walked around and saw no sign of the boy

Suddenly Bert pointed. "Look, Nan!" he exclaimed. "There he is, talking to that man!"

As the twins approached they were amazed to hear the man thunder at the boy:

"No, I haven't a job for you. Now get out!"

CHAPTER XIX

SAM GETS A HELPER

HANGING his head, Biff Rand turned away from the man who would not give him work at the wild animal show. Bert had started to dash toward Biff, but Nan caught her brother's hand.

"Take it easy," she said. "Don't accuse Biff of being a thief till we know more about it."

"But we are sure of it," said Bert.

Nan said they could probably learn much more by being kind to Biff. Bert shrugged and told her to go ahead and see what she could do with him.

As the suspected boy walked off sadly, the twins hurried up to him. Just before they reached Biff, he turned his head. Seeing the two, a look of fright came into his eyes and he started to run.

"Please wait!" Nan begged. "We want to talk to you."

Biff did not stop running. Bert and Nan took off after him. Since Biff was larger and could run faster, the twins were fearful that he would get away from them.

"We only want to talk to you," Nan called. "Please stop. We're not going to tell the police on you."

Nan's last sentence seemed to do the trick. Biff began to slow down and finally stopped. But when he turned to face the twins, a look of defiance came over his face.

"I'm in a hurry, so make it snappy," he said.

This remark angered Bert and he started to speak. But Nan poked him in the ribs and Bert said nothing.

"Biff," Nan began, "I went to see your mother the other day."

"What! You know my mother?" Biff cried.

Nan nodded. She said Mrs. Rand wanted her son to come home at once, no matter what his reason was for staying away. She was very distressed and lonely.

"But I can't go home," Biff said. "I—I—"

The poor boy could not go on. It seemed to Nan as if there were something he wanted to say, but found it hard to do so.

"Yes, I know," said Nan kindly. "You didn't want your mother to support you any longer, so you ran away from home to take care of yourself. Perhaps you planned to send her some money when you got it. But you found it impossible to get work, and so you—"

"No, that's not the way it was," said Biff. "Two men came through our town. They said they were looking for a boy to help them take care of their wild animals. They wanted to know if I'd like to apply for the job. I did."

Biff went on to say that he had been with the men only a few days when they discharged him. He did not know the reason. He thought he was doing all right. That was why he had come to this wild animal show—to get work.

"Everything went wrong," said Biff. "Then I—I took something I shouldn't have and after that I was afraid to go home." He looked at Nan intently. "You're telling me the truth about my mother, aren't you?" he asked.

"Indeed I am," said Nan.

Bert spoke up. "Biff, did you take anything except my bicycle and some magazines?"

Biff looked startled that the Bobbsey twins knew about the magazines. He said these and the bicycle were the only things he had taken.

"I just can't go home until I have some money," he said. "I'm not going to take another thing in my life. But I'm not going to let my mother support me, either. I'll go home, but not till there's something in my pocket."

He started to walk away, but the twins detained him.

"Listen, Biff," said Bert, "did you tell it around Lakeport that Danny Rugg was the one

who hit my little brother Freddie with the bike,
so you wouldn't be blamed?"

Biff looked blank, then he said, "I don't know
what you mean. I didn't hit your brother and I
don't know Danny."

Bert and Nan were sure he was telling the
truth. After a moment Biff said:

"I rented your bike to a boy named Ben Terra
to do an errand. He must have hit Freddie.
When he brought the bike back, the headlight
was gone. I went looking for it, but I only found
some broken glass."

"That's when we saw you," Bert said. "Ben
must have started the rumor about Danny. He's
a mean guy."

Once more Biff started to move away. Quickly
Nan whispered to Bert. Then she dashed off.
Her twin went up to Biff and laid a hand on the
other boy's shoulder.

"I know you're proud and you don't want to
accept things from people," he said, "but I was
just going over to have some ice cream. Nan
doesn't want any. Will you join me?"

Biff looked at Bert suspiciously, but the Bobbsey twin smiled in a friendly way. Biff finally
smiled faintly himself and said he would join
Bert. The two walked over to the ice cream
stand.

In the meantime, Nan had hurried to a telephone. She put in a call to her father and

explained what she and Bert had found out.

"Couldn't Biff work in your lumberyard, Daddy?" she asked.

Mr. Bobbsey chuckled. "You're at it again, I see. Well, bless your heart, Nan, I'm glad you're helping someone. If you think it's all right for me to offer this boy a job, I'll be glad to do it."

"Oh, Dad, you're wonderful!" said Nan.

"Somebody really ought to help Sam on his truck," said Mr. Bobbsey. "I think that would be a good place for Biff to be. Sam could keep an eye on him."

Nan hung up and hastened back to where the boys were eating double ice cream cones.

"I have something very exciting to tell you, Biff. I was just talking to my father on the phone and he says you may work for him helping with the lumber," she said.

Biff Rand stared at Nan as if he could not believe what she was saying. She repeated the offer, saying that Biff was to help Sam on the truck. Suddenly Biff wiped his eyes with the back of one hand. With a catch in his voice, he said, "That's awfully decent of you kids. And your father too. I don't deserve it."

"Of course you do," said Nan. "Anybody who wants to work should be able to find a job."

Bert was pleased with the arrangement. In the few minutes that he had been alone with Biff, he had changed his mind completely about the boy. He was a good sort and Bert knew that he felt exceedingly bad about having been dishonest.

"Do you think your father would agree to pay me by the day?" Biff asked suddenly. As Nan nodded, he went on, "With my first day or two's earnings I could pay back those people whose magazines I took. Then I can start returning all the money Dave Parks gave me on your bicycle, Bert."

Nan smiled, and said she would speak to her father. She was sure he would agree. Then she said:

"If you haven't any plans, Biff, how about coming home with us? You should meet the rest of our family right away."

Biff immediately looked at his shabby appearance. He said that he had not been able to keep looking neat because he had been sleeping outdoors practically every night since he had run away from home. He had been soaked by the rain a couple of times and his clothes had suffered.

"I'm sure Dad has a suit you can wear," said Bert. "Come on!"

Biff did not argue further. He became very quiet, hardly able to believe that he had fallen into such good luck. He willingly followed the twins to the car and was introduced to Sam. At once Nan told him the new arrangement and

Sam welcomed the boy as a helper. The kindly colored man did not mention that he knew of Biff's dishonesty.

Biff sat in the rear seat with the twins. After they had driven a few minutes, Biff began to tell about a few of his experiences.

"Those two men I told you about were named Joe Shunter and Al Caster. They had a house deep in the Manfred Forest."

"That's not so very far from here," Bert remarked.

"No, it's not," said Biff, "but it's very wild. They had a stockade and said whenever they brought animals there, they kept them in it."

Bert asked if there were any animals when Biff had gone there. He said no, but that the men had expected to bring some very soon.

"One day they took me into Lakeport and told me they would pick me up the next morning. They were going on a little trip to get an animal. The next day they came back with a bear in their horse van."

"Was its name Bobo?" Nan asked eagerly.

Biff looked surprised and said yes, that was the bear's name. Nan and Bert looked at each other. They decided not to tell Biff that the bear had been stolen.

"They took me as far as a little restaurant and gave me something to eat. Then they told me to go on back to Lakeport, that they were all

through with Manfred Forest. I came to town
and got to the school just as another bear was performing. After everyone had gone inside the
school, I saw your bike on the grounds, Bert. I
just couldn't resist the temptation to take it and
sell it. I was going to send the money to my
mother, but when I couldn't get any work, I had
to use it for food."

Bert asked Biff if he knew anything about the
bear which had been tied to the school fence and
left alone. Biff said the animal was still there
when he had gone off with the bicycle.

"Why, did the bear run away?" he asked.

The twins told Biff about the mysterious disappearance of Hugs, and explained that they
did not know whether he had wandered away
or had been stolen.

By this time Sam had reached the Bobbsey
home. Nan hurried in ahead to warn the small
twins not to say anything to Biff about his having stolen anything. They promised not to.
Biff came into the house slowly. The others
realized it was difficult for him to face them
all, but the entire Bobbsey family and Dinah
were friendly.

Everyone had eaten except the older twins,
so Dinah fixed three places at the table. While
she was getting supper ready for Nan, Bert, and
Biff, Mr. Bobbsey and his older son took Biff
upstairs. While their visitor was taking a bath,

they found him a complete set of clothes. The
trousers were too long, but when they were
turned up, Biff looked very well dressed in
them. After supper, Mrs. Bobbsey came and sat
down beside the boy.

"Would you like to stay with us overnight?"
she asked.

"You're too good to me," Biff said. "I'd like
to, but I don't think I should."

Mrs. Bobbsey said it would not put them out
at all. There was no extra bed in the house, but
there was a very comfortable bedroom over the
garage. They would be very glad to have Biff
use it. Finally the boy accepted. After a while,
Bert took him over there and left him. When
the twin came back inside, his mother smiled
and said:

"I suppose I might have tucked Biff into the
house some place. But I thought it best if we did
not make him feel as if we were watching him.
It's up to him now to make good. We've given
him every chance."

Flossie and Freddie wanted to know exactly
what she meant. Their mother smiled and said
that by morning, they would have their answer.
If Biff really wanted to work and pay his debts,
they would find him still with them. If he were
not the right sort, she felt sure he would run
away during the night.

The Bobbsey twins wondered what would happen. When morning came, each of them was awake early. They all met in the kitchen.

"Bert, you go and find out if Biff is still here," Freddie urged.

CHAPTER XX

RIGGING AN ALARM

HOPEFULLY Bert Bobbsey climbed the stairs to the second floor of the garage. Would Biff Rand still be there?

The door to the bedroom was closed. Bert knocked. At first there was no answer and the Bobbsey twin was fearful that their visitor had left. But when he knocked a second time, a sleepy voice said:

"Come in!"

What a relief it was to see Biff Rand lying on the cot!

"Time to get up," said Bert cheerfully.

"Gee, I'm glad you called me," Biff said. "This was the first good night's sleep I've had in so long, I couldn't wake up."

Bert told him to come over to the house for breakfast, then left the boy. He hurried back to tell the others the good news that Biff was still there. Dinah smiled and said she would fix sausages and flapjacks for breakfast.

Everyone enjoyed the delicious meal and then

left the house for their various tasks. Biff Rand's face shone as he set off for the lumberyard. The Bobbsey twins were very happy. Only one thing happened all day to mar its cheerfulness. Charlie Mason told Bert at lunchtime that Danny was spreading a story around school.

"He says you Bobbseys are boarding a thief," Charlie announced.

Bert was so angry to hear this that he went after Danny in a hurry. But Danny was careful to keep out of Bert's way. When Nan heard the story, she advised her twin not to fight and get into trouble. She reminded him that the next day they were going to Big Bear Pond. It would be too bad if Bert had to stay behind because of any punishment by Mr. Tetlow.

"I guess you're right," Bert admitted, "but Danny sure burns me up."

His twin remarked that few people ever believed what Danny said, anyhow. She thought it was silly to worry about this latest attempt of Danny's to make trouble for the Bobbseys.

Late that afternoon Biff came home ahead of Mr. Bobbsey and Sam. He asked Bert and Nan if they would help him do something.

"Your father paid me for my work today," he said. "It's more than enough to cover the price of the magazines I took. Will you go around with me to those houses where I sold the magazines and see if I can get them back?"

Bert and Nan readily agreed, and the children had no trouble gathering the magazines. Biff promised to deliver them to the people who should have received them from the postman. He explained that he had seen the pile of magazines on a front porch, not realizing at first that they belonged to the postman.

"The rest of the money I've earned I'll send to my mother," Biff added. "Every day I'll take out only what I need for food and my room and send everything else to her."

Bert and Nan were delighted to hear this and said they would see him when they returned from Big Bear Pond.

Since there was only a half day's session at school next day, the twins were packed and ready to leave at one o'clock. Sam drove them to Nada Bergen's house to pick up the little girl, then they set off.

When they reached the animal reserve, Freddie and Flossie immediately dragged Dinah and Sam to Kisses' cage. The bears recognized the twins and began to tumble and dance.

Later the twins unpacked their bags, then Bert went to ask Grandpa Bergen if they might start rigging up the alarm system.

"I'm all ready. I bought the wires and batteries and bells yesterday," the old man said.

Freddie wanted to know if he could help, and

Freddie and Flossie dragged Dinah and Sam to Kisses' cage

proudly joined the two others when they said he might. The three worked for the rest of the afternoon and started in again first thing the next morning. Soon the system was ready to be tried out in one section.

"Please let me set off the alarm," Freddie begged.

Grandpa Bergen smiled and said he might. Freddie put a ladder alongside the gate to Kisses' enclosure. The alarm had been rigged to the latch, which was too high up for him to reach from the ground.

"Ready?" he called.

"Ready!" Grandpa Bergen replied.

Freddie slid back the bolt on the fence gate and lifted the latch.

Burrrrrr!

"It works! It works!" the little boy shouted in glee.

In his excitement Freddie had leaned too far over on the ladder on which he was standing. The next second, it teetered. The little boy clawed the air, but this did not help him. He and the ladder fell to the ground!

Bert and Grandpa Bergen ran forward. They quickly helped the little boy to his feet and asked if he felt all right.

"I—I guess so," he said, trying to keep back the tears. The tumble had knocked the wind out of him and this made his chest hurt a little.

Bert suggested that Freddie go back to the house and take it easy for a while. It would not take long to attach the alarm to the other enclosures. In a short time the job was finished. When Grandpa Bergen and Bert came back to the house, Freddie declared that he was feeling all right again.

In the meantime the girls had had a lot of fun, and now everyone was very hungry. They sat down to a delicious supper which Dinah had enjoyed preparing.

"We're goin' to have a little bear dessert," she announced as she removed the plates from the table after the main course.

"What kind of dessert is that?" Freddie wanted to know.

The cook merely smiled. But when she brought in the dessert, everyone else smiled too.

"Biscuits and honey!" Freddie shouted. This was a favorite of his.

Bert ate several of the biscuits and when he finally left the table with the others, he declared he felt as fat as a bear looks. Grandpa Bergen laughed and said that if Dinah prepared meals like this all the time the children were staying there, he would be sure to gain several pounds.

"We children better not get any fatter," Nada spoke up, "or we won't be able to get into the cave. It's pretty narrow."

At once the twins wanted to know when they

were going to make the trip to the spooky cavern. Nada said if they wanted to, they might all go the following morning.

"Oh, let's do!" said Freddie.

Directly after breakfast the next morning Grandpa Bergen handed Bert a big flashlight. He said the children were to go nowhere else except the cave. It was a fairly long walk and they were all to put on their hiking shoes.

"Is that on account of snakes?" Flossie spoke up, wondering if she really wanted to go.

"Yes," Grandpa Bergen replied. "And also rough stones and lumpy ground."

As the group started off, Flossie held tightly to Nan's hand. But presently she began to be a little ashamed of herself. Nada was only a wee speck older than she was, and Nada was not afraid of snakes or anything else. The little girl was leading the way, half walking and half running toward the cave.

"It's right up ahead," she announced fifteen minutes later.

The Bobbseys could see the opening now. It was large, but as they entered, the cave immediately became small. Bert and Nan could easily touch the top with their hands and there was very little room on each side of them as they walked along.

Presently Nada stopped and said, "Listen!"

The Bobbseys could hear nothing but dripping water. Flossie began to shiver. This was a little spookier than she wanted the trip to be.

A moment later Nada started on again. In a few minutes the cave grew a little larger and the children could walk side by side. Again the leader paused.

This time Flossie clutched Nan, terrified. She did not know what the sound was that she heard, but it seemed to her like moaning and groaning.

"Wh—what's that?" she whispered to her older sister.

"Don't be frightened, dear, it's only the wind," Nan replied.

Bert beamed his light around the walls. The rocks were of many colors and very pretty. Here and there water dripped down over them. Suddenly the children heard a whirring noise. A second afterwards something whizzed over their heads and they all ducked.

"Oo-oo!" Flossie exclaimed. "Nada, I want to go back!"

Nada laughed. Her voice sounded hollow and echoed back to them.

"We're not even halfway through the cave," she told Flossie. "There's nothing to be afraid of. That was only a bird."

Nada had barely finished speaking when the children heard another sound ahead of them. Looking directly forward, they were startled to see two bright eyes staring at them!

CHAPTER XXI

A SCARE

THE TWO large eyes continued to stare at the Bobbsey twins and Nada Bergen. They knew the eyes belonged to some wild animal. Would it spring at them any moment?

"Let's run!" Flossie screamed, turning around and dashing off in the opposite direction.

"Stop!" Nan called after her, knowing the little girl would get lost in the inky darkness.

Bert, overcoming his first fright, beamed his flashlight ahead at the animal. Its ray would not quite reach, so slowly the boy walked forward.

"Bert, don't do that!" Freddie advised. He was shaking like a leaf.

But his brother continued to walk forward. As he drew closer, the light finally showed up the rest of the animal.

"*An owl!*" Bert exclaimed.

All the children burst into laughter. This aroused the owl, which began to blink at them.

"Say," said Freddie, "do owls sleep when their eyes are open or shut them when they're awake?"

The little boy's mixed-up question made the others laugh harder than ever. This seemed to disturb the owl. If he had ever been asleep, he certainly was awake now. He gave a loud "To whoo!" which reverberated through the cave, causing the children to clap their hands over their ears.

A moment later, the owl took off from his stony perch and fled from the cave.

"Ooh!" said Flossie. "I'm glad he's gone and I hope we won't meet any more wild animals in this cave."

Nada laughed and said she could promise nothing. But surely no animals were in the cave to really hurt the children. She herself liked these spooky adventures.

"I guess I will, too, when it's all over," said Flossie with a sigh.

As they walked along, Nada said they would soon come to the surprise. She would not tell the children what it was and let them guess. They guessed a waterfall, an underground river, a bear's den, and a rock garden.

"No, you're all wrong," their little friend replied.

Presently they came to a sharp turn in the cave. As Bert flashed his light around the corner, the twins gasped. Before them lay a miniature fairyland.

Icicles had formed themselves into a pattern which looked like a fairy castle. In front of it were several other icicles that seemed like tiny figures.

"There's my favorite," said Nada. "Doesn't that look just like a man on a horse?"

"You mean an old-fashioned man?" said Flossie. "What do you call him?"

"A knight," Nan replied.

The Bobbseys picked out other figures. Flossie declared one looked just like Little Red Riding Hood on her way to see her grandmother.

"It looks as if all the nursery rhyme people were here," said Nan after gazing at every figure. "That one over there is like the old witch on a broom, only she's so white."

The children stayed in the spot a long time, looking at the fascinating sight. But finally Nan said they should go. It must be almost lunchtime.

"I have one more surprise," Nada told them as they walked on. "Maybe we won't get out of here."

Before Flossie and Freddie could become frightened, Bert said quickly, "Is this another one of your jokes, Nada?"

The little girl laughed and admitted that it was. The surprise was the funny way in which

they would have to get out. One had to bend almost double like a snake to make it.

"Big people can't do it," she said, "so when
they come to the cave they have to go out the
other way."

"I'm glad I'm little," said Freddie, "because
I want to pretend I'm a snake."

When they reached the end, Nada went first
to show the others how to bend their bodies in
order to pull themselves out. It turned out to be
a real trick. It was not too hard for Flossie and
Freddie, but Nan and Bert just managed to
make it. As a matter of fact, as Nan tried to
straighten up, she found it a bit difficult.

Laughing, she said, "Ouch! My back feels as
if it were all full of kinks!"

Freddie looked up at his sister. "You're not a
very good snake, are you?" he said. "Why don't
you get on the ground and wriggle around like
one? Maybe that'll fix your back."

The kink in Nan's back did not improve, so
she decided to try Freddie's suggestion. On the
ground she twisted this way and that. The others
laughed, but the motion made something in
Nan's back click. In a moment she stood up, saying she felt all right again.

They reached home just as Dinah was ready to
serve luncheon. The twins told her about the
cave and said they wished she might see the fairy

castle inside it. But Dinah decided she was much too stout and had better not go in for fear she would never get out.

Late that afternoon the children helped Grandpa Bergen prepare a treat for the animals. He called it "bear pancakes." Actually it was honey spread on large, thin rice cakes. Nan and Flossie took the treat to Kisses, Honey, and Beesy.

When they entered the animals' cage, Kisses and her cub, Honey, came up to get some of the food. But Beesy, who was lying on the ground some distance away, did not move.

"Come on, Beesy!" Flossie cried. She picked up

one of the rice cakes, walked over to Beesy with
it, and laid it on the ground. The baby bear
sniffed at the cake but would not touch it.

"Oh!" Flossie cried in alarm. "Beesy's sick!"

Nan hurried over to see whether Flossie was
right. She leaned down and felt the little bear's
nose. It was very hot! Nan knew that this was
what happened to all animals when they are not
feeling well.

"Beesy *is* sick," Nan said. "We'll get Grandpa
Bergen at once."

Reaching the gate, they saw the elderly man
coming. Flossie begged him to hurry.

"Poor Beesy is awful bad off," she told him.

The bears' owner opened the gate and came
inside. He hurried over to the cub and began to
examine him. He felt the little bear's legs and
head and back. He announced that nothing was
broken.

"I'd say," Grandpa Bergen said, "that Beesy
needs some salt."

Grandpa Bergen explained that all wild animals need salt. He perhaps had been neglectful
in bringing any to this cage recently. He hurried
off and brought back a large cake of salt. Almost
as soon as he laid it down by the ailing cub,
Beesy began to lick it.

"I'm sure the little fellow will be all right in
no time," Grandpa Bergen prophesied.

The girls wondered if Kisses and Honey

would stop eating the rice cakes and lick the salt. But for the time being, the two bears were too busy with the delicious food to bother with it.

Grandpa Bergen left the cage, but they all came back about two hours later to see how Beesy was feeling. To their delight, the little bear was walking around and seemed much better.

"By morning he'll be fine," Grandpa Bergen assured the children.

When they returned to the house, the girls heard Bert talking on the telephone. He called the other twins over and said that their mother and father would like to speak to them.

When Nan spoke to her mother, she was delighted to hear that Biff Rand was making out extremely well. He was working hard, and Mr. Bobbsey liked him very much.

"What's even better than that," said Mrs. Bobbsey, "is that Biff has had a letter from his mother. She is so happy that everything is turning out nicely and she can hardly wait for him to come home. He's going to visit her on Sunday."

"Oh, that's lovely," said Nan, who was very happy, too.

Before it was time for bed, Flossie and Freddie suggested that they all play a game of charades. The little twins had been whispering together, and Bert and Nan knew that they had

something funny which they wanted to do. The
small twins insisted, however, that Bert and Nan
do a charade first.

The older twins whispered a few moments,
then they walked out into the middle of the
living room. Nan started saying, "Moo!" with
Bert walking behind her. For a few seconds the
others could not guess. Then suddenly Freddie
called out:

"I know. Cowboy!"

"That's right," Nan laughed, and the older
twins sat down.

Now it was Nada's turn. She did an excellent
pantomime. When it was finished Nan called
out:

"Are you Old Mother Hubbard?"

Nada said she was. Then she sat down. Instantly Freddie and Flossie got up. They disappeared into the kitchen, and when they returned
a moment later they had Dinah with them.

"Dinah's part of our act," Flossie announced.

The cook seated herself on the couch. Instantly Flossie and Freddie climbed onto her
lap. Then they began to hug her very hard.
At once Dinah made a gurgling sound which
finally ended in a whistle.

Freddie and Flossie began to giggle and
rolled off Dinah's lap. They turned toward the
others in the room, and said:

"What are we?"

Nada and the older twins could not guess. But suddenly Grandpa Bergen began to laugh.

"I think I know the answer," he said. "Are you a pressure cook—er?"

"Oh, you're a good guesser!" Flossie cried.

Everyone laughed heartily as Dinah got up. She said, "Those children sure pressed me hard. And now I think all of you should get to bed."

The twins soon fell into a deep sleep, but sometime in the middle of the night, they all were rudely awakened. Each of them got out of bed and listened.

The alarm on the bears' cages was ringing wildly! Was someone trying to steal the bears?

CHAPTER XXII

A NEW CLUE

"COME ON, everybody!" shouted Bert Bobbsey from the hall of Grandpa Bergen's home.

He had put on his moccasins and a bathrobe,
and already was dashing down the stairway.
Freddie and the girls put on their slippers and
robes and followed him.

Grandpa Bergen was in the lower hall, talking excitedly. He was pointing to the buzzer of
the alarm system.

"It's Kisses' cage!" he exclaimed.

He unlocked the door and rushed outside with
the children in pursuit. The moon was shining
brightly, so they were able to hurry ahead without the use of flashlights. Bert and Grandpa
Bergen, however, had each slipped one into their
pockets. Dinah had gotten up also, but had taken
time to put on some of her clothes. It was not
until they had reached Kisses' cage that she
caught up to them.

"Lawsy me, what's happened?" she asked, worried.

Grandpa Bergen explained that he thought they had just gotten to the cage in time to forestall a theft. Kisses and her cubs seemed to be very much excited.

"Oh, I'm so glad those bad men didn't take you!" Flossie cried out.

Nada said she was glad, too. The little girl loved this mother bear and her children more than any others in the reserve. Now she went inside the cage and began to talk to them.

Bert asked Grandpa Bergen whether he was sure the men had left or were only hiding. After the searchers went into the house, perhaps the men would come back.

"They probably will," said Grandpa Bergen. "Bert, suppose you and I comb these woods to be sure they've gone."

Freddie wanted to go along, but Dinah thought it best if the little fellow stayed with her. He was beginning to shiver from the chill of the woods, and she did not want him to catch cold.

Nada came out of the cage again, and the alarm was set once more. Grandpa Bergen arranged it so that it could not be turned off except from the house.

"Don't you want us to wait here at the cage while you look around?" Nan spoke up.

Grandpa Bergen shook his head. He said

there was no point in the girls and Freddie getting cold, and he doubted that the men would
come back while they knew a search was on.

"I'll tend to 'em," Dinah promised. "Just let
me catch those fellows comin' back here to take
your bears!"

Dinah suddenly looked so fierce that Grandpa
Bergen smiled. He said he knew she would certainly be able to take care of things. He and Bert
turned on their flashes and started off through
the woods. They took a zigzag course, beaming
their lights in every direction. There was not a
sound, and they did not catch sight of anybody
hiding.

After they had been hunting through the
woods for half an hour, Grandpa Bergen
thought they should give up. He was sure the
men had become frightened and run off.

"They may try it again tomorrow night, but
I doubt that they'll come back tonight," he said.

Bert could not agree. He felt that men as determined as Shunter and Caster would probably
make another attempt.

"Are we near a road?" he asked Grandpa
Bergen.

"Why yes, we are. We're not far from my
private lane."

"You mean the one where we found the horse
van?" Bert wanted to know.

"Yes."

"Then let's look along the lane," Bert said. "We might find the van."

Grandpa Bergen reminded him about the blockade, but Bert insisted that this would not keep out a determined driver. They hurried along the lane and, to Mr. Bergen's amazement, found the van!

As they went forward cautiously, Bert whispered, "Do you think one of your stolen bears is inside?"

"No telling what we may find," was the reply.

But the van was silent and empty. Grandpa Bergen decided that this was a case for the police. They must hurry to the house and telephone headquarters. Bert suggested that they let the air out of the tires to prevent the men from escaping in the van.

"Good idea. And we'll drain the gasoline tank, too," Grandpa Bergen said with a chuckle.

When they arrived back at the house, Mr. Bergen telephoned the police. Afterward he told the children that the state police had investigated Manfred Forest but had found no trace of Shunter and Caster, nor of Hugs or Bobo.

"If any of them were ever there, they've skipped out like they told Biff," he said.

After Dinah served cocoa and cookies to all, the children retired for the night. Grandpa Bergen decided to stay on the first floor to be ready to run outside, should the alarm go off.

But the alarm did not sound again that night.

"Do you think one of your stolen bears is inside?" Bert asked

In the morning, when the children came downstairs, Grandpa Bergen said he already had
heard from the police.

"Oh, what did they say?" Freddie asked
eagerly. "Did they catch the bad men?"

"No, unfortunately they didn't," Grandpa
Bergen replied. "The police went at once to the
van, but the men did not come there. Probably
we scared them off. The police took charge of
the van, so at least for a while those men won't
be able to steal any of our bears."

"Hurray!" cried Freddie and, in his exuberance, got down on the floor and turned two
somersaults.

Nan asked whether the police were sure that
the van belonged to Shunter and Caster.

"Yes, it does," Grandpa Bergen replied. "The
license was in the name of Joe Shunter."

During breakfast Nan was very thoughtful.
She hardly said a word, and finally Dinah asked
her if she felt well.

"Oh, yes," Nan answered quickly. "But I've
been thinking about something. Maybe we can
find Bobo and Hugs ourselves."

Grandpa Bergen said he would be glad to
listen to any plan. It was really a great loss to
him financially not to have Bobo and Hugs to
sell.

"Do you mean, Nan, that you have a hunch
as to where they may be?" he asked.

"Yes, I have. If Biff was right about those men keeping their wild animals in Manfred Forest, maybe they didn't take them away at all. If they found the police were after them, they may have run away before they had time to take the animals somewhere else."

"But the police searched thoroughly, and there were no animals in the cages," Grandpa Bergen said.

"I know," said Nan, "but the animals might have gotten loose. Or Joe Shunter and Al Caster might have set them free."

Grandpa Bergen stared at the girls. Then he said:

"You could be right, Nan. I suggest that we go and find out. We'll start right after breakfast!"

CHAPTER XXIII

THE HONEY TRAP

AN HOUR later the little group was ready to start their trek to Manfred Forest. Grandpa Bergen carried a bear's collar with him and also a heavy chain.

"Here's something for you to carry," he said to Nan, handing her a bag. "Don't drop it. It'll break."

Nan peeked into the package. It contained a large jar of honey. She smiled and asked if this were part of Grandpa Bergen's way of trying to find Bobo and Hugs. He admitted that it was.

"I shan't use it unless I have to," he said.

He did not explain further, and the Bobbsey twins were curious to know how he could make use of the jar of honey. They did not ask, because just then Dinah spoke up.

"I hope you have big success," she said, smiling. "I'll keep my fingers crossed. And don't you all worry about this place. I'll take good care of it. If that alarm goes off, I'll telephone the police right away."

"That's fine, Dinah," said Grandpa Bergen, as he went toward his horse van.

All the children climbed inside. The small twins sat in the cab with Grandpa Bergen, but the others thought it would be fun to ride inside.

"I just hope this won't be a wild goose chase," said Nada's grandfather with a sigh.

Suddenly Nan held up her hands and crossed the fingers on both of them. Nada did the same, and finally, Bert, with a chuckle, crossed his fingers too.

"Let's hope we have that success Dinah was talking about," said Nan seriously.

When they reached Manfred Forest, Grandpa Bergen was forced to park the van at the edge of it. There were no roads running among the trees. As they all got out and started walking, Flossie said, "Ooh, this is a black forest."

The others agreed that the tall trees which grew close together made it seem very dark indeed. What a wonderful place for wild animals to live in!

The trekkers had not gone very far when suddenly they heard a crow begin to caw loudly. Almost at once, birds started to fly from the trees and shoot upward from the forest.

"Why are they doing that?" Flossie asked.

"Old Mr. Crow is guardian of the forest,"

Grandpa Bergen explained. "Whenever he thinks there's danger, he warns all birds. I suppose he thinks we're hunters."

"But we're not," said Flossie.

"Sure, we are," Freddie spoke up. "We're hunting for bears."

The others laughed and said Freddie was right. They walked for some time until they were deep in the forest. Then Grandpa Bergen stopped and began to call loudly:

"Bobo! Hugs! Where are you?"

Hopefully the children listened, but there was no answering sound.

They walked farther and repeated the call. This time the children helped. Still no bears appeared.

"I guess I'll have to resort to the honey," Grandpa Bergen said. "Nan, will you open it, please?"

Nan took the jar from the bag and unscrewed the lid. Then she handed the jar to Grandpa Bergen.

To the children's surprise, he poured half the contents of the jar on a fallen tree trunk. Then he said:

"Let's hide!"

He and the children dodged behind near-by trees. Then he explained that bears seemed to be able to smell honey from a great distance. If Bobo or Hugs were in the forest, surely they would come to get the honey.

As the Bobbsey twins and their friends waited, they were amused at visitors to the log. First came a squirrel, which sniffed at the sweet stuff, and then ran away. Next came a cute little chipmunk. He did not seem to like honey either.

By this time several birds had returned to the forest. Apparently they had been told by the old crow that the girls and boys and their leader were harmless people. One by one the birds swooped down to sample the honey. They did not seem to care for it particularly, and flew away.

"Oh boy, look what's coming!" Freddie cried out. "Bees!"

A whole swarm of them suddenly descended on the log. What a buzz they made! Some alighted on the edge of the log and reached in to get the honey, but others flitted just above it, reaching down with their tiny proboscises into the sweet, sticky mass.

"There won't be any left for the bears if they do come," Flossie giggled.

The watchers were so intent on looking at the bees that they did not notice the approach of an animal until suddenly twigs cracked beneath its feet. Hearing it, everyone turned.

A bear was approaching!

All the children wanted to shout in glee, but Grandpa Bergen put one finger over his lips to indicate silence. Slowly the bear ambled toward the log. Reaching it, he gulped down two or three of the bees and the rest of the swarm flew away. Then the bear began to lick the honey.

In a moment Grandpa Bergen stepped from behind the tree and tiptoed toward the bear. As he clamped the collar about the animal's neck, he said:

"Bobo!"

The children expected the bear to be pleased, and started to come from behind the tree. But to their horror, Bobo was quite unfriendly. He stood up on his hind legs and gave Grandpa Bergen a hard cuff with his paw.

"Bobo! What's the matter with you?" his owner cried, dodging a second blow.

Grandpa Bergen moved back, but kept tight hold of the chain. Suddenly Bobo gave a loud *whoof* of rage and tried to yank away.

"I'll help!" Bert exclaimed, picking up a heavy stick.

Seeing this, Nada cried out, "Don't use that! It'll only make Bobo worse."

Bert dropped the stick and stood still. Nada slowly walked forward toward the bear.

"Hello, Bobo!" she said in a soft voice. "Have you forgotten Grandpa and me?"

The bear dropped to his forefeet and looked at the girl. She continued to advance, holding out her right hand in a friendly gesture.

"Come here and let me scratch your nose," she said.

Suddenly Bobo became very docile. He sat down on his haunches and held up his right front paw to Nada. Laughing, she ran forward and shook it hard.

"I guess you had your freedom for so many days, you didn't want to come back, did you?"

As if he knew what the little girl was saying, the bear shook his head vigorously from left to right. Now the Bobbsey children ran forward, laughing.

Grandpa Bergen came closer to Bobo. He waited until he was sure Bobo would mind him, then said they would all start for the van.

Nan said to the bear, "Is Hugs in this forest, too?"

Of course she did not expect an answer, but, to her amazement, Bobo once more shook his head as if he were saying, "No."

"I think we'd better get Bobo back to Big Bear Pond, anyway," said Grandpa Bergen. "We can come back later and get Hugs if he's here."

Bobo went along with them gladly and in a short time was inside the van. The cage in which he had been kept was not far from Grandpa Bergen's private lane, so they drove into the reserve this way. Bobo was led into his cage, and then the group took the shortcut to the house.

As they neared it, Flossie said, "Won't Dinah be s'prised? Freddie, come on, let's run and tell her!"

The small twins raced ahead. They started calling the cook's name before they reached the house. But she did not answer them. They hurried inside and looked all around. Dinah was not in any of the first-floor rooms and did not respond to their repeated calling.

By this time the others had arrived and also were amazed that Dinah was not there. Nan suggested that perhaps the cook was resting. She would go up to her bedroom and find out.

But Dinah was not in her room, either. The Bobbsey twins looked at one another in dismay. Dinah was a person who always kept her word. Whatever could have taken her from the house?

Flossie began to cry. "Something awful's happened to Dinah," she sobbed.

CHAPTER XXIV

DINAH'S ADVENTURE

GRANDPA BERGEN was not worried about Dinah. He said she certainly was old enough to take care of herself.

"If Dinah left the house, it was for some very good reason. Perhaps Sam came and took her out for a ride," he said.

At this remark, the Bobbsey twins shook their heads vigorously. They all insisted that Dinah never walked out on a job. She had said she would guard the house and grounds, and would not have left them unless something very unusual had happened.

"Maybe the phone isn't working," Nada suggested, "and Dinah went to get the police."

Freddie had been silent for some time. Now he said in a woebegone voice:

"I'm terrible hungry. I thought Dinah would have lunch ready."

"I'll get you all something to eat," Grandpa Bergen offered. "And I'll tell you a little story while I'm cooking it."

Bert and Nan looked at each other. They knew the kindly man was doing this to keep the small twins from worrying about Dinah. It was a good idea, so Nan did not even offer to help. After Nada and Freddie and Flossie had followed Grandpa Bergen into the kitchen, Nan went up to her twin.

"Don't you think we ought to hunt for Dinah?" she asked.

"Yes, I do," Bert agreed. "Nan, you know what I think happened?"

"What?"

Bert led his sister to the alarm system in the hall.

"I think this has been tampered with. Dinah may have seen someone around the grounds trying to cut the wires, and followed him."

Nan looked frightened. Maybe something *had* happened to Dinah!

"Let's hurry!" she cried and dashed from the house. As Bert followed, he asked where she was heading. Nan said she was going directly to Kisses' cage. If Joe and Al had come back to steal one of the bears, she was sure it would be Kisses.

As they approached the cage, the twins were delighted to see that Kisses and her two cubs were still in it. There was no sign of Dinah, however. But when Bert and Nan walked to the far side of the cage, they saw her hiding behind a tree.

"Dinah! You gave us such a fright!" Nan exclaimed. "What are you doing here?"

"I'm guardin' this place till the police come," she said staunchly.

The faithful cook explained that while she was working in the house, she suddenly had heard voices outside. Hurrying to a window, she had been just in time to see two men sneaking off among the trees.

"One of them was saying, 'Nobody's here now but that dumb old woman. Now's our chance to take a bear.' "

Dinah pulled herself up proudly. "So I said to myself, I'll just show those folks I'm no dumb old woman," she added, fire in her eyes. "I'm gonna keep them from stealin' a bear if it's the last thing I do!"

Dinah went on to say that the other man had mentioned cutting the alarm wire from Kisses' cage before they tried to take her.

"What did you do then?" Nan asked.

"I phoned police headquarters right away," Dinah replied. "Then I came out here to guard this place. I don't know whether the men got scared or whether they're gonna come back later. Anyhow, I haven't seen hide nor hair of them."

Bert and Nan were amazed at the whole story. Bert said he would help Dinah guard the place, but she thought this was too dangerous. If the men should come back before the police arrived,

they might hurt Bert, and she would never for-
give herself.

"Old Dinah's big and strong," she boasted. "I
won't let them hurt me!"

Nan said she thought Grandpa Bergen should
know what was going on. She wanted to run back
to the house and tell him. Dinah insisted that
Bert go too. There was no arguing her out of it,
so the twins started back.

They were only halfway to the house, when
they heard a loud scream. *Dinah!* What had
happened?

Turning about, the twins raced back to Kisses'
cage. At first everything looked peaceful. But as
they ran behind the cage, they saw two men
standing by Dinah. One had his hand over her
mouth and the other was getting ready to tie a
handkerchief across it. He also was bringing a
rope out of his pocket. Apparently he was going
to tie Dinah to the tree!

"You quit that!" Bert cried out.

The men looked around but went on with their
work. In a trice, Dinah was roped to the tree
with the handkerchief across her mouth.

The children began to fight the men but were
no match for them. Both were large and very
strong.

"So you kids want the same treatment, eh?"
one of them yelled as he brought more rope from
his pocket.

Bert and Nan were in a panic. What if they too were tied up and the men ran off with Kisses before help came!

Just as they were wondering what to do, they heard twigs snapping in the woods. Grandpa Bergen and the small children came racing toward the cage. The two men, knowing that it was impossible now for them to carry out their work, started to run. But though they were fleet-footed, the Bobbseys and their friends were even quicker. With Grandpa Bergen and the five children after them, it was impossible for them to escape.

Fists flew as the men still tried to get away, but finally they were subdued. Both were thrown to the ground, and the children and Grandpa Bergen sat on their chests.

The two men scowled and one of them said angrily, "We haven't done anything! You can't keep us prisoners!"

"You were going to steal a bear," said Grandpa Bergen. "And you've already stolen two of my bears. Where is Hugs?"

The other man sneered. "Try and find out!"

The Bobbsey twins were stunned. They had caught the men responsible for taking Hugs, but this was not going to return the beautiful bear to Grandpa Bergen.

Suddenly Bert exclaimed:

"I have an idea!"

CHAPTER XXV

A CELEBRATION

EVERYONE waited to hear what Bert Bobbsey's idea was. Facing the men squarely, he said
unexpectedly:

"What boat did you ship Hugs on?"

The men were so stunned at his question that
before they thought, both replied, "The *Colum-
bia.*"

Bert Bobbsey's idea had worked! The men
had confessed!

Since they had given themselves away, the two
thieves admitted everything. They said that they
were indeed Joe Shunter and Al Caster. They
had orders from several European circuses to
obtain trained bears. Hugs had not actually been
shipped yet. They had had very good luck until
they met the Bobbsey twins.

"You're smart kids, all right," Joe owned up.
"Too smart!"

The children grinned, and Grandpa Bergen
praised them for what they had done to help

him. Then he asked Joe and Al where Hugs was at this moment. They gave the name and address of a friend in New York.

"Suppose we go up to the house now and you telephone your friend," Grandpa Bergen suggested. "Tell him to ship the bear back here at once. And don't try to get away."

Joe and Al, completely beaten, made no effort to escape. Walking in front of the others, they went to the house. At Kisses' cage, the little group halted long enough to untie Dinah. She scowled at the two men and shook her finger.

"I'm sure glad you got caught!" she said. "I hope you go to jail and live on bread and water."

"You're really the one who's responsible for the capture of Joe and Al," Grandpa Bergen told her.

Dinah smiled happily. She said she was always glad to help folks out.

Just as they all reached the house, the police drove in. They waited until Joe Shunter had made the telephone call to New York requesting the return of Hugs. Then they took charge of the two prisoners and drove off with them.

After Bert and Nan had eaten lunch, Dinah served dessert to everyone, saying, "I think the twins should have a party to celebrate, now that the mystery is solved."

Grandpa Bergen agreed. "We'll have it here day after tomorrow. And a bear party, too!"

Quickly plans were made. The guest list would include Mr. and Mrs. Bobbsey, Biff Rand, and Nada's parents. Since Nellie Parks and Charlie Mason had helped solve the mystery, they were invited. Freddie and Flossie asked Susie Larker, Teddy Blake, and Sally Smith.

All the next day the twins helped tidy the grounds and prepare the food. Finally the time arrived, and the guests drove in.

The twins greeted Biff, who told Bert he had found out who started the story about Danny knocking Freddie off his bike.

"It was Ben Terra," Biff explained. "He looks

something like me, I guess, so I got the blame."

After a delicious luncheon, the guests pulled their chairs into a circle. Then the show began. How the guests loved it!

At the end of the show, Grandpa Bergen said he had a surprise. He explained that just before the show had begun, he had received a telephone call.

"Hugs is arriving in a cargo plane at an airport a few miles from here. Would you like to go and meet him?"

"Yes, yes!" they all chorused.

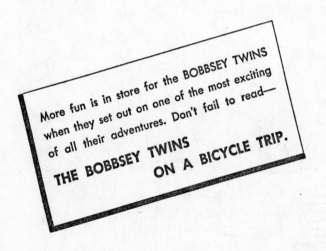

More fun is in store for the BOBBSEY TWINS when they set out on one of the most exciting of all their adventures. Don't fail to read—

THE BOBBSEY TWINS ON A BICYCLE TRIP.